My name is Jack Fairfax. Twenty-one years old. Formerly of the Royal Flying Corps. Actually, I'm Lord Fairfax, but that's something I'm still taking time to get used to. Today the bells of our village church are ringing out to tell everyone that the armistice has been signed. The Germans have surrendered. The War is over. I'm at home here in Oxfordshire on this day, rather than with my former comrades in France, because two months ago my fighter plane was shot down while battling the Hun. I was invalided out of the Corps and sent back to England with a broken leg and a broken arm. I had got off lightly – unlike so many of my friends. Particularly my best pal, Alan Dixon. But to get the whole story, we have to go back to 1915, and our last days at school...

The wind whistled as Alan Dixon and I clung on to the roof with our fingernails. Because it was dark we couldn't see the ground below, but we both knew it was a long, long way down.

It had seemed such a good idea at the time. The last day but one at school for me and Alan, my best friend, called for something special to celebrate it. The curtain was coming down on long years of self-important prefects, bullying masters, and four centuries of "school traditions" rammed down our throats at every opportunity. The occasion merited more than just attending the final assembly, singing the school song, and shaking hands with masters and housemasters we'd come to loathe before we went on our way.

That's when I'd suggested hanging a pair of trousers from the steeple at the top of the school chapel. Many years before when my grandfather, who was also called Jack Fairfax, had been at this school, he'd done the same sort of thing, using one of the master's mortarboards.

"If we do it at night no one will see so no one will know it was us," I said.

Alan laughed. "Of course they'll know it was us," he replied with a grin.

"You know how this school operates," he said. "Gossip and sneaking."

I shrugged. "So what if they do know," I said. "It's our last day here. What can they do? Expel us? Anyway, this place deserves something to liven it up."

And so I'd sneaked into the laundry room and snaffled a pair of trousers belonging to our housemaster, Mr Stokes, a short, balding, humourless man and my personal enemy during most of my years at school.

Now, at eleven o'clock at night, Alan and I were on the last leg of our climb, and I, for one, was starting to have second thoughts about it.

The first part had been easy – up to the top of the chapel, and out through a skylight on to the roof. The second part was more difficult – climbing up the slippery slates towards the steeple. Luckily Alan had thought to bring a couple of screwdrivers he'd picked up from somewhere, and we used these to dig into the slates to get some kind of leverage. As it was, it took us about twenty minutes just to get to the ridge at the top of the roof.

We were working our way along the ridge, me sitting astride it as if I was riding a horse, Alan more elegantly crawling along it on hands and knees, when suddenly Alan lost his grip on the slimy tiles and slid. In the darkness I heard his hands trying to clutch at the tiles, but the speed at which he fell made getting a grip impossible. I heard a crashing sound from the bottom of the roof, and then Alan calling, "Jack! Help!"

I was already halfway down the roof, but I was taking it slow so I didn't lose my grip. Alan had gone over the edge of the roof and was hanging by his fingers from the guttering. Below him was a drop of a hundred feet. There was no way he would survive if he fell.

I put my foot into the gutter, reached down and grabbed one of Alan's arms.

"Can you kick with your feet to push yourself up?" I asked.

"There's not much to kick against," said Alan.

I steadied myself, then reached with my other hand and took a firm grip beneath Alan's armpit.

"I'm going to try and haul you up on the count of three," I said. "Ready?"

There was a terrible creaking from the guttering, and Alan said, "I'd make it 'two' if I were you."

I didn't bother to count, I just pulled with all my strength. It felt as if my arms were being wrenched out of their sockets, but then Alan gave a kick which must have connected with something out of sight, and his head and shoulders appeared over the gutter.

I hauled him in, like landing a particularly heavy fish, and Alan lay balanced on the roof, getting his breath back.

4

"Thanks," he said. "I thought I was a gonner then."

"You can't die yet," I said. "We're supposed to go and fight the Hun together, remember?"

Alan grinned. "True," he said.

That was our plan. Finish school and then go off to the War together. We were both 17, nearly 18. Alan and I had been best pals ever since we'd met at our prep school when we were both six years old. We'd been put into the same dormitory because our names were next to each other on the school roll, Dixon and Fairfax, and somehow we'd remained close chums ever since.

We even used to swap clothes if one of us had problems with something like a rugger shirt that needed cleaning, but we'd forgotten to get it washed. It helped that we were about the same height and the same build. The only real difference between us was that Alan had dark, curly hair, while mine was a mixture of fair and reddish brown.

"It's going to be difficult getting to the top of the steeple with the slates as slimy as this," said Alan.

"Well we're not abandoning the plan now," I said, determinedly.

"Of course, it depends how we define the 'top' of the chapel," said Alan. "It doesn't have to mean the steeple or the top of the bell-tower."

"That's a very good point," I said. "In fact, it'll be even harder for Stokes to get his trousers back if we hung them from the end of the ridge than if we hung them from the steeple. After all, they can get into the bell-tower from inside."

"So, we're decided then," said Alan. "The trousers hang from the ridge."

"But at the end," I said, "so they can wave in the breeze like a flag."

I gave Alan a concerned look. "Are you sure you want to risk going up on to the ridge again?" I asked.

"Of course," said Alan indignantly. "I can hardly fall off again a second time. What sort of idiot do you think I am?"

"The sort of idiot who comes up here in the first place," I replied.

We began to clamber up the greasy slates again, only this time taking more care, moving more slowly. Finally we made it to the ridge of the roof, and I pulled Stokes's trousers from where I'd loosely fixed them around my waist, and Alan and I tied them firmly into position.

"There!" I said triumphantly. "We are flying the flag of freedom!"

The summons came next morning. Alan and I were in the rooms we shared, packing our things ready to go home, when there was a knock at our door. It was Padwith, one of the school servants.

"Good morning, Mr Fairfax, Mr Dixon," he said. "Mr Stokes says he wishes to see you in his study."

"Very well, Padwith," I said. "Tell Mr Stokes we're on our way."

"Looks like they've noticed the trousers," said Alan ruefully. "I think we're going to get a beating."

"It won't be the first one," I said. "I might as well leave this school keeping up my tradition of being beaten at least once a month."

Alan hadn't been beaten as much as I had during his time at school, and he gave me a quizzical look.

"Don't you mind being beaten all the time?" he asked. "Frankly, I hate it. That cane cutting into the flesh of one's behind. It hurts like hell."

"I think of it as preparing me for life outside school," I said. "Dealing with pain without showing it hurts. When I'm over there, fighting the Hun, and they take me prisoner and start torturing me, I shall just look them straight in the eye and say, 'Do your worst! Nothing you can do can ever be as painful as my years at school!'"

Alan laughed. "We could always refuse to go and see Stokes," he suggested. "After all, it is our last day at school. What can he do if we don't turn up, but just leave?"

"Nothing," I replied. "But I won't give him the satisfaction of telling other people I was a coward because I refused to face him and take my punishment."

Alan sighed.

"I suppose you're right," he said. "It still irks me that that little bully is allowed to thrash me. In a fair fight I'd knock him down with two punches."

Alan and I finished our packing, strapped up our trunks, and then walked slowly together across the quad to Stokes's study in the masters' block. I knocked on his door.

"Come in!" called Stokes.

I opened the door and Alan and I stepped in.

I was very familiar with Stokes's study, having been summoned to it pretty often during my time at school, usually to be told off, and to be beaten. It had a smell I thought I would always remember: the strong tobacco from Stokes's pipe hung everywhere – in the curtains, in the books, in Stokes's clothes. Then there were the dusty bookshelves. I'm sure that Stokes sometimes took a book from his shelves to read, but most of the books seemed to have a fine film of dust over them. The only clean smell came from the scent of polish on Stokes's desk. His servant spent hours polishing and waxing the top of it.

Stokes was sitting behind his desk, and he stood up as Alan and I came in. His face was creased with distaste, as if he was suffering from a stomach upset.

"Fairfax and Dixon!" he scowled.

"Sir," we responded.

Stokes came round from his desk and stood in front of us, glaring. I suppose it was meant to intimidate us, but as he was shorter than both Alan and myself, it wasn't very successful.

"I understand that you two were responsible for that dangerous and stupid prank last night, involving climbing the roof of the chapel," he began.

"It wasn't really dangerous –" I began, but Stokes cut me short.

"Silence, Fairfax!" he snapped. Turning to Alan, he said in an angry tone, "Fairfax's action I can understand, to a degree. He has been ill-disciplined and a troublemaker almost from the first day he came to this school. But you, Dixon. You have a fine academic record. Your behaviour is usually a credit to the school, and to your family. Why, Dixon?"

"It was my fault, sir," I said. "I led Dixon astray in this matter. The responsibility is totally mine."

Stokes turned to me, his little eyes boring into me.

"When it is your turn to speak I will tell you," he said. "I am talking to Dixon." Turning back to Alan, he again demanded, "Why?"

Alan hung his head.

"I am sorry, sir," he said. "I have no excuse. And it was not Fairfax's fault. I was as responsible as he was for climbing the roof. It just seemed a nice thing to do to celebrate the end of school."

Stokes said nothing, but just looked at Alan for a moment. Then he asked sarcastically, "A nice thing?"

Then Stokes turned to me.

"So, Fairfax," he said. "You have decided to end your days at this school in the same way you have spent them. With an irresponsible act and contempt for authority."

There didn't seem much point in saying anything to that, so I didn't.

"Your brother, Oswald—" Stokes began, and I gave out a silent groan. It obviously hadn't been silent enough, because Stokes glared at me.

"You have something to say, Fairfax?" Stokes demanded menacingly. "Something important enough to consider it worth interrupting me when I am addressing you?"

"No, sir," I replied.

Stokes glared at me again, and then began praising my wonderful older brother, something both he and my father did whenever I had been caught doing something I shouldn't.

"Your brother, Oswald, was a perfect pupil when he was at this school. Disciplined. Courteous. Dedicated."

Don't I know it, I thought ruefully. Everyone tells me often enough. At 19 years old, Oswald was two years older than me. At school he'd won every prize, excelled at everything, and had been head boy before he left.

"Where is your brother now?" Stokes demanded.

The question puzzled me. I couldn't see what on earth Oswald's location had to do with me about to get a beating. Especially as Stokes knew very well where Oswald was and what he was doing.

"He's with the Royal Scots Dragoon Guards, sir," I said. "On the Western Front. Fighting the Hun."

Stokes nodded. "Exactly," he said. "And what do you think he would say if he heard about this latest escapade of yours?"

I thought about that, then said, "Not a lot, to be honest. I think he'll be too busy watching out for German bombs to worry about me climbing a chapel spire."

Out of the corner of my eye I saw Alan stifle a grin. Stokes breathed in and out harshly, his face twitching, like a bull getting ready to charge.

"I suppose you think that's funny," he demanded. "No, sir..." I began, but Stokes stopped me.

"Your brother is risking his life, putting his King and

ountry, the good name of the school and the Empire before himself, as always, and you make a joke about it!" he stormed angrily.

"No, sir," I protested.

"Do not answer me back!" Stokes snapped. "During his time at this school Oswald was always a good example to the other boys. You, on the other hand, have been a bad example. You show disrespect for many of the masters, who are your elders and betters."

Elders, but not necessarily betters, I thought to myself, but I decided not to say anything. It was my last day at school and I was in enough trouble already. Stokes would be reporting everything I said back to my father and mother. In this situation I decided it was best just to shut up, take my punishment, and put it all behind me as soon as possible.

Stokes stood looking disapprovingly at us both for a few seconds more, then said, "It causes me great pain to beat any boy on his last day at school, but the act you perpetrated cannot go unpunished. For me to ignore such an offence would send out a wrong message to the rest of the school. The other boys here would consider it gave them licence to commit every act of folly on the last day of school, and that is not going to be the case!"

Stokes walked to the umbrella stand, where he kept his cane. He took it out, flexed it, and then returned to where we were standing.

"Dixon," he ordered, "bend over the chair."

As Alan walked over to the upright chair in the corner of the study, I spoke up.

"Sir," I said. "I think I should be beaten first. After all, I was the person most responsible."

Stokes gave me a hard look.

"I know you think you are being chivalrous, Fairfax," he said. "You believe that whoever gets beaten first will be beaten the hardest, because my arm will tire by the time I beat the second boy. I must assure you, that will not be the case. I have enough strength in my arm to beat you a hundred times if necessary, and each stroke as strong as the last."

With that he strode to where Alan had bent himself over the chair. Stokes pulled back the cane, and then launched it hard at Alan's backside. Whack! The sound of cane on cloth and flesh echoed around the room. I saw Alan bite his lip to stop himself yelling out against the pain. Whack! Whack! Six times the cane thudded into Alan, and each time he took it without uttering a sound.

After the sixth stroke, Stokes stepped back.

"You may stand now," he said.

Alan stood up and turned to face Stokes. Alan's face was white and there was a bead of sweat on his forehead. In the time-honoured school tradition after a boy had been beaten, Alan held out his hand towards Stokes.

"Thank you, sir," he said.

Stokes said nothing, just took Alan's hand and shook it.

"You may go," he said. "I will, of course, be writing to your father about this."

Alan nodded, and then – with a last sympathetic look back at me – left the study. Stokes flexed the cane between his hands, and then gestured towards the chair.

"Fairfax, take the position," he ordered.

Dutifully, I went to the upright chair and bent over it, tensing myself against the pain that I knew I was about to experience.

There was a pause, then a swishing sound as the cane cut through the air at speed, and I felt a pain like fire across my buttocks, even through the flannel of my trousers. The swine was being as true as his word – he was hitting me as hard as he'd ever hit me in all my time at school.

Swish... Whack! The second stroke bit even harder than the first, and I clenched my teeth, biting on my lip to try to offset the pain.

Swish... Whack! Three strokes. Three to go. Whack!! Whack!! Whack!!!

As the sound of the sixth stroke echoed around the study, I straightened up and turned to face Stokes, but he barked in a fury at me, "I have not given you permission to stand up, Fairfax! I have not yet finished!"

I was shocked. Six strokes of the cane was the standard punishment.

For a second I was tempted to defy him, to grab the cane from him and break it, and then set about him. But I controlled myself. I would not give him that satisfaction. Instead, I nodded as calmly as I could, turned, and bent over the chair again.

Whack! Whack! Whack! Whack! Another four blows landed on me, each one hurting more than the last as they landed on skin already beaten and cut by the previous blows.

After the tenth stroke, I waited, still bending over the chair, determined not to be caught out again by Stokes. "You may stand now," said Stokes. His voice was hoarse and contorted, and I realized at that moment that he really hated me.

I stood up and turned to face him, and, traditional as ever, held out my hand to him. Stokes glared at me, then he took my hand.

"Thank you, sir," I said, and then I began to squeeze his hand.

The look on Stokes's face became one of shock as he realized that I wasn't just shaking his hand, but grasping – hard. I felt him try to pull his hand away from mine, but my grip was too strong. I clutched harder, and now Stokes tried to squeeze back, fighting against my grip, but I was younger and fitter – stronger. Beads of sweat appeared on Stokes's forehead as he struggled to fight against the crushing pain I was sure he was feeling in his hand, but I kept a firm hold.

I don't know how long we stood like that, all the time our eyes locked on each other as we fought this silent battle. It could only have been a minute at most, but it felt like an eternity. Finally, Stokes whimpered, his eyes closed, and he croaked out hoarsely, "You're hurting my hand."

Immediately I let his hand go.

"My apologies, sir," I said.

He stood there, rubbing his crushed right hand, rocking slightly back and forth on his heels. "May I go now, sir?" I asked politely.

"Yes," he said, through clenched teeth. "Thank you, sir," I said. And with that, I left.

I spent the rest of the day going around the school, saying goodbye to my chums and making promises to meet up some time in the future. The general feeling was that we'd be meeting up next on the fields of Flanders in Belgium and France, as soon as we'd gone through Royal Military Academy at Sandhurst and become officers and joined our various regiments. Nearly everyone had someone who was out there fighting the Hun, either an elder brother – as was the case with me and Oswald – or a cousin, or an uncle.

"My father's got my commission already sorted out for the lancers," one pal, Martin Wickham, told me, adding, "I suppose you'll be joining the Greys and your brother out on the Front."

I shook my head.

"Not me," I said. "I'm going to get my wings and join the Royal Flying Corps."

Wickham looked at me, shocked.

"Flying?" he said.

"That's right," I said nodding. "That's where the future of warfare lies. Up in the skies. Alan Dixon and I are planning to go in together.

Wickham frowned.

"What does your father say about that?" he asked. "I bet he's not keen."

"I haven't told him yet," I said. "I'm going to tell him as soon as I get home."

At 3.30 p.m. on the dot, school was officially over for Alan and me, and the school servants hauled our trunks and bags down from our rooms to the lobby, where we waited for our respective drivers to take us home.

"Still up for joining the RFC?" I asked.

Alan beamed and nodded happily.

"You bet!" he said. "I'm going to start making arrangements for flying lessons as soon as I get home."

"Same here," I said. "I can't wait to get over to France and start bombing the life out of the Hun. That's what this war needs. Young people like us with new ideas. That's what's going to win it. Not treating it like it's the Hundred Years War all over again."

Just then I saw the family car coming down the drive. "Ah,

here's my ride!" I said. I held out my hand and Alan and I shook hands firmly.

"I'll be in touch tomorrow, as soon as I've told Father what I'm intending to do," I said.

"Hadn't you better wait a day or two for the dust to settle?" suggested Alan. "What if he doesn't give his permission?"

"I don't need his permission to learn to fly," I said. "And if the old skinflint refuses to pay for the lessons, I've got some money of my own put by. Nothing's going to stop me, Alan, that's for certain."

Even as I said it, I knew I faced trouble over this flying business when I got home. Wickham was right about my father. He would definitely not be keen. The men of the Fairfax family had always served Britain and the Empire by joining the Greys, more properly known as the Royal Scots Dragoon Guards. Even though our family had lived in Oxfordshire for over a hundred years, we had strong Scottish connections. In fact, the family name, Fairfax, is Scottish.

Within the Fairfax family, the Greys were known as "the Regiment" and unless a male Fairfax was intended for some other profession, such as the law, medicine, or the church, that was where he went. The Regiment had been formed in 1692, and in 1693 the cavalry began riding grey horses, hence the Regiment's nickname. As you can see, it was a long tradition.

The drive back home to Bowness Hall, just outside

Oxford, was quiet. Meadows, the servant who'd been sent to collect me and take me home, had been with the family for twelve years. He'd been with us since Father had become Lord Fairfax on the death of my grandfather, the previous Lord Fairfax – which had also made me the Right Honourable Jack Fairfax.

Meadows was a nice fellow of about 40 who lived with his wife and three children in a cottage on our estate. As we drove, I pumped him for information to catch up with how things were at home.

"How are my parents, Meadows?" I asked.

"Lord and Lady Fairfax are very well, Mr Jack," answered Meadows.

"And Nanna?"

"Lady Margaret is now in good health, I'm pleased to report," Meadows replied. "She had, as you may know, a touch of bronchitis three months ago, but I'm glad to say that it has cleared up. The recent dry weather seems to have been advantageous to her in that respect."

Lady Margaret, known more affectionately to me as Nanna, was my father's mother. She used to be Lady Fairfax until my grandfather died, and then, as the widow of the previous Lord Fairfax, she became known officially as the Dowager Lady Fairfax. My mother had then become the new Lady Fairfax. But, to avoid confusion, Nanna decided it would be easier all round if everyone called her Lady Margaret.

Nanna was possibly my favourite person in the whole family. She was gentle and never told people off. If a servant broke something or did something wrong and Father started to give one of his lectures (usually accompanied by a threat of dismissal "if it happens again"), Nanna would often intervene on the servant's behalf, pointing out how honest and reliable the servant usually was, and how they deserved to be given at least another chance. Nanna would sometimes even take the servant below stairs and offer them a drink of brandy or something to "help them recover from the awful experience". This annoyed my father enormously as he believed Nanna was undermining his authority and discipline when she acted in this fashion. Father was very strong on "authority and discipline".

"Any news from Oswald?" I asked Meadows. I hadn't heard directly from Oswald since he went out to the Front with the Regiment four months earlier. Not that we'd ever been that close as brothers. Oswald tended to take Father's view that I lacked discipline and was a bit too mischievous.

"Mr Oswald's most recent letter to your parents was about a month ago," said Meadows. "As I understand it, he is in good health, considering the conditions out in Flanders."

"And what are the current conditions out there?" I asked. "We've been a bit cut off from things about the War at school, to be honest. The head and the staff tell us we're winning but we have to pray for victory. When any of the boys get letters from the Front they're all marked out in black, where they've been censored. All in all, it's hard to find out what the situation is. Are we really winning the War?"

Meadows was silent for a moment, then he said, though I thought I caught a cautious note in his voice, "The newspapers and the government say we are, Mr Jack."

"Ha!" I said. "No one believes them. What do they say in the village?"

"Opinions are divided, Mr Jack," said Meadows. "There are some who say it'll all be over by Christmas. Then there are some who say it's going to be a long war. There's lots of talk about the new weapons the Germans are using. Particularly this poison gas."

I nodded. Even at school we'd heard about that. Just three months before, the Germans had launched an attack against the Allied forces at a place called Ypres in Flanders. This was the second attack they'd launched on that small town, which was right on the front line between the two armies.

In November 1914 the Germans had tried to smash through the British and French lines at Ypres. The British and French had stopped them, but at a tremendous cost to the Allies. We'd heard stories of 60,000 British and another 60,000 French dead, compared to 150,000 Germans dead. Since then there'd been a stalemate at Ypres, until this new attack in April. This time the Germans had launched a gas attack against the British, Canadian and French forces holding the town, before the actual assault. One of the boys at school, Owen Lewis, told me his uncle had been caught up in it.

"He said a blueish-white mist just came rolling towards them from the German lines," Lewis told me. "At first no one knew what it was. Thought it was just a fog of some kind." It turned out to be chlorine gas. Thousands of men choked to death as the gas hit them. Some, like Lewis's uncle, were left blind and had to be invalided back to England. The Germans, wearing gas masks, made their attack a few hours later. Seventy thousand British, French and Canadians died in that attack.

Luckily, according to another fellow at school, the Canadians, wearing makeshift gas masks made out of wet towels, counter-attacked and pushed the Germans back.

It was when I heard these kind of stories that my mind conjured up pictures of my brother and I wondered what he was doing. How was he coping with it out there? He'd obviously not been caught up in anything like that, or we would have known about it, I was sure.

As we drove the rest of the journey to Bowness Hall, I pumped Meadows for more local gossip: who was doing what in and around the village, who'd joined up in the army, who was poaching, that sort of thing.

It was about eight o'clock when we finally rolled up in front of the Hall. While Meadows unpacked my belongings from the car, I went up the steps to the house. Mother was waiting for me at the top, and from the strained expression on her face I could tell straight away that something wasn't right.

"What's wrong, Mother?" I asked. "Is it Oswald? Has there been bad news?"

Mother shook her head. "No," she said. "As far as we know, Oswald is well."

"Nanna?" I asked.

Although Meadows had told me that Nanna was in good health, there was no denying she was old and frail.

"No, Jack. Your grandmother is well."

I frowned, puzzled. "Then what has happened, Mother?" I asked.

"Your father wishes to see you in the library," she said.

The penny dropped. Stokes must have phoned Father and given his version of what had happened.

"Ah," I said.

Mother wrung her hands mournfully and said in a whisper, "Why do you always have to get into trouble, Jack? You know it upsets your father."

"I'll explain to him," I said.

As I set off for the library, I knew that it would be a waste of time trying to explain anything to Father. But, just for once, I thought I'd try. Father was pacing up and down in the library as I entered. He stopped pacing when he saw me.

"You wanted to see me, Father?" I said.

The grim expression on his face told me that this was going to be a repeat of my interview with Stokes, though without the beating at the end of it, I hoped. My bottom was sore enough already from the ten whacks Stokes had given me.

"I had a telephone call today from your house master," he said.

"Ah," I replied.

"Is that the best you can say!" he thundered angrily. "No," I said. "I tried to tell Mr Stokes I was continuing a family tradition, but he didn't want to listen."

Father gaped at me, as if he couldn't believe the words he was hearing.

"Family tradition?!" he snapped.

"Yes, Father," I nodded. "Nanna told me that when Grandfather was at school, he climbed the chapel steeple and hung one of the masters' mortar boards from it. I thought it would be fun to do what he did."

Father glared at me for a second, then turned and started pacing up and down again, as if he was having a battle inside himself about what to do next.

My father saw himself as being a pillar of respectability in his role as Lord Fairfax, a shining example to the villagers and everyone else. He didn't like to be reminded that his own father had been a bit of a practical joker, with a reputation for getting up to all sorts of mischief.

Finally, he stopped pacing and turned to me again.

"I would prefer it if you discounted stories that your grandmother tells you about your grandfather. She is elderly and prone to exaggeration."

"But he did climb up the chapel steeple at school," I said. "I heard it from one of the old servants there, as well."

"Whatever your grandfather may or may not have done in his youth, he grew out of that foolishness as he grew older," said my father sternly. "You have brought shame on our family name by carrying out this particularly stupid, dangerous and irresponsible escapade on your very last evening at school. It is how you will be remembered."

I jolly well hope so, I thought. Mad Jack Fairfax, daredevil.

"I just hope that you won't embarrass Oswald in this manner when you go out to join the Regiment. Assuming, that is, that the War isn't over by the time you get your commission."

This is it, I thought. There's no time like the present.

"Actually, Father," I said, "I won't be joining the Regiment."

Father looked at me, and his mouth fell open in shock.

"What?" he said, stunned.

"Alan Dixon and I have decided to join the Royal Flying Corps. We're going to learn to fly and get our wings, and fight the Hun that way."

Father continued to gape at me as if I was talking to him in some foreign language.

"The Royal Flying Corps?" he echoed.

"Yes," I nodded. "One of the chaps at school, Chuffy Liddle, his brother's in it. Sounds awfully exciting. Lots of chances to actually meet the Hun face to face and shoot them down."

Father was opening and closing his mouth as if he was trying to breathe, then finally said, "Absolutely not! Positively out of the question! Aeroplanes! Toys! This is war, boy!"

"Exactly, Father," I agreed. "And it's going to be won or lost in the air. The side that controls the skies is going to be the one that wins this war. That's what the papers said. And that's where I'm going to be – up there!"

Father looked at me hard, then he shook his head and gave a deep groan.

"I don't know where I've gone wrong with you, Jack," he said. "Maybe it's not me. Maybe it's your mother. Or the masters at school being too soft on you."

I thought of Stokes and his cane and gave a wry smile.

Father shook his finger at me firmly.

"There's only one place for a Fairfax at a time like this, when the country's in peril, and that's in the Greys, at the forefront of the action. Not skulking like some coward in the skies, away from the battle."

I bridled, annoyed at this.

"It's hardly away from the battle, Father," I protested. "The Hun firing at you from the ground with anti-aircraft guns. Their planes attacking you. There's nowhere to hide in a plane. There are no trenches to take cover in up in the skies."

Father said nothing at first. He simply glared at me as if the power of his stare alone would force me to change my mind. But he didn't understand me. I was no longer a little boy who could be threatened with a beating. I'd had beatings for most of my life, and they hadn't changed a thing. I was rising 18 and as tall as my father – I could look him straight in the eye and tell him how I felt and what I wanted to do. I'd left school, and I refused to be treated like a schoolboy any longer. I was my own man.

Father carried on glaring at me, but when I didn't buckle he shrugged and turned away from me.

"You may go to your room," he said. "We'll talk sensibly about this idiotic idea of yours tomorrow, and hope you will come to your senses."

As I left the library I felt a sense of pride in myself. It had been a good day. I'd been beaten for the last time by Stokes, and held my pride with him. And I'd refused to be brow-beaten by my father. Jack Fairfax was going to be making his own mark.

In fact I didn't go to my room. Instead I arranged with cook to serve me up a meal later on, and then I went to pay a visit to Nanna.

Nanna had her own quarters in the west wing of the Hall, with her own staff: her own housekeeper, Mrs Johnson, and her own maids, Milly and Dolly. It was Mrs Johnson who opened the door to Nanna's rooms when I knocked, and her face lit up when she saw me.

"Master Jack," she said smiling. "Her ladyship was hoping you'd call. She said to show you straight in when you did. Would you like tea?"

"Tea would be lovely, thank you, Mrs Johnson," I said.

Mrs Johnson went along the corridor in front of me, skirts flapping like a ship in full sail, and rapped on the door of Nanna's sitting room before going in.

"Master Jack, your ladyship," she announced.

Nanna was sitting in one of the big comfortable armchairs in her sitting room, reading a book, which she put down as soon as I came in.

"There you are!" beamed Nanna.

I hurried over to her and gave her a kiss, and then sat myself down on the settee near her.

"What's this I hear about you being a naughty boy again, Jack?" she said.

"I wasn't really naughty, Nanna," I said. "Just a bit of a daredevil. I wanted to do what Grandpa did when he was at school, so I climbed the chapel spire."

"Yes, I'm afraid you do have your grandfather's naughtiness and high spirits, but not much of his brains," said Nanna sternly, though I could see a twinkle in her eye as she said it. "Your grandfather also did well in his exams, something I understand you don't follow him in."

I gave a sigh. "That's true, Nanna. Anyway, enough about me. How are you? How's your health?"

Nanna smiled. "Not good enough for me to climb up a chapel steeple, but enough to keep me alert to what's going on," she said. "I hear that you've upset your father, and you've only been home five minutes."

"Oh well, you know Father," I shrugged.

"I know him well enough to know how upset he'd be with this idea of yours of going into the Flying Corps." I gaped at her, stunned. "Nanna, you are truly amazing!" I said. "I've only just told Father, and then I came straight here! How did you find out so soon? I swear, in the old days you'd have been burnt as a witch."

Nanna gave a small, sly smile. "Walls have ears, and I listen to them."

Of course. The servants. Our servants had obviously overheard my conversation with my father. In turn that had been passed on below stairs to other servants, and either Milly or Dolly would have picked it up and passed it on to Mrs Johnson, who would have passed it on to Nanna. And all in the space of a few minutes. In a large house, servants need to know what's going on: who's in a good mood and who's in a bad mood, or when large sums of money are owed to tradespeople. All these things affect their position. As a result, the "bush telegraph" is usually faster than any telegram.

"I take it you're serious about this flying business?" asked Nanna. "It's not just a whim to annoy your father?"

I shook my head. "I'm absolutely serious, Nanna. I

know it will mean that Father won't talk to me for weeks. Maybe months. But I've heard about this war and what's happening, and the way to win it is in the air. And I'm going to be there, in a plane, fighting for our side."

Just then, Mrs Johnson came in with a tray. As she poured our tea out for us, I asked Nanna, "Do you think I'm letting the family down? After all, Grandpa was a hero of the Regiment as well."

"No, no," replied Nanna. "Your grandfather loved the Regiment, but it wasn't the be-all and end-all for him. No, it was the men of the Regiment who were most important to him. The soldiers who served under him. That's the difference between your father and him. Your father loves the history of it. My Jack loved the people in it."

She sipped at her tea, then said, "Did you ever hear about Christine Welsh?"

I frowned, puzzled. "No," I said. "Who is she?"

"Was," corrected Nanna. "She was in the Regiment." This puzzled me even more.

"What as?" I asked. "A cook? Washerwoman?" Nanna shook her head. "She was a soldier," she said. I laughed. "Oh come on, Nanna!" I said.

"It's absolutely true," said Nanna. "Your grandfather told me about it."

"Then he was having you on," I said. "Playing a joke." Again, Nanna shook her head.

"I checked," she said. "All the facts were right. You can ask your father, if you like. He won't like admitting it, but it's true."

I was intrigued. A woman fighting as a soldier in the Greys? It was impossible. Women simply weren't allowed in the Regiment.

"It was back in 1702," said Nanna. "This woman, Christine Welsh, had married a man who'd joined the Regiment and gone off to war. Unlike most women, who just stay behind and get on with their lives, Mrs Welsh set off to find her husband. She dressed herself as a man and called herself Christian Welsh, and joined up in the Regiment to look for him."

"And no one noticed?" I said, incredulous.

"Not for four years," said Nanna.

"Did she find this husband of hers?" I asked.

"Oh yes," said Nanna. "But he was killed in active duty, so she carried on serving as a soldier until she was seriously wounded in the Battle of Ramillies, I believe it was, in 1706. It was while the surgeon was fixing her up that he noticed that she was not what she appeared to be."

"Four years, and no one spotted her! It doesn't say much for the eyesight of the soldiers in the Greys."

"No, but it says a lot for Mrs Welsh's courage," said Nanna. "She broke the tradition of the Regiment, and she proved her worth as a soldier."

I looked at Nanna quizzically, still not completely sure she wasn't playing a joke on me.

"I'm sure there's a point to this story, Nanna," I said. "But, I must admit, I don't see what it is."

Nanna smiled. "It's about not thinking in straight lines," she said. "You don't have to live by everyone else's rules, but you can't just challenge them. You have to go along with them, at least part way, if you want to get what you want. Christine Welsh didn't try and join the Regiment as a woman. She wouldn't have got in."

"So how does this affect me and Father?" I asked, still puzzled.

"Your father is a good man, but he thinks in straight lines," said Nanna. "If you want him to see things differently, you have to go along those straight lines with him at first, before you start to move off and go on different roads."

"You think I ought to go into the Regiment," I said gloomily.

"No," said Nanna. "I think you ought to offer your father the chance that you will."

"But I can't do both," I said. "I can't join the Flying Corps and join the Regiment."

"You can tell him that you'd like to give the Flying Corps a try first. And, if it doesn't work out, then you promise to join the Regiment."

"He won't accept that," I said. "Father's very firm in his views."

"He might accept it if he realizes that you're going to join the Flying Corps anyway, with or without his permission. This way he doesn't lose face. As far as he's concerned, you're still going to join the Regiment. But later, once you've got this flying nonsense out of your system."

I sat there, tea cup in hand, and thought about what she said.

"You are very clever, Nanna," I said.

Nanna smiled and nodded. "I know," she said.

Next morning over breakfast I tried out Nanna's suggestion on my father. To my surprise, he agreed. He didn't agree at first, obviously, and it took some pretty hard talking on my part to persuade him. He only finally gave his begrudging agreement after I'd given him my word that, if I couldn't get into the Royal Flying Corps, or if I did and made a mess of it, I would immediately try for a commission in the Greys.

I telephoned Alan straight after breakfast and told him the news.

"Well done!" he said.

"How about you?" I asked. "Have your parents agreed?"

"No problem there," he said. Alan came from a different sort of background from me. His father and grandfather had been merchants and so he wasn't stuck with a family history of riding in cavalry ever since the horse had been invented.

"Right," I said. "Let's go and join up."

"Ah, that's not so straightforward," said Alan. "What do you mean?" I asked.

"We got in touch with the RFC yesterday, but it seems they're full up at the moment and they can't take any more people on for training."

My heart sank. All that arguing with my father, persuading him, and now it looked as if I wouldn't be able to get in to the Flying Corps after all.

"Hello?" came Alan's voice in my ear. "Jack? Are you there?"

"Sorry, Alan," I said into the phone. "It's just that you gave me a bit of a shock. I've promised my father that if I can't get into the Flying Corps I'll join the Regiment, and now you tell me they're full up."

"Only at the moment," said Alan.

"Yes, but that won't be any use when I tell my father why I'm not going straight off to join up. He'll insist I keep to my promise and go into the Greys."

"It doesn't mean we can't learn to fly," said Alan. "In fact it would be a good idea for us to get some basic training. The chap I spoke to at the RFC said it would make us more likely to be accepted into the Flying Corps when we do get the chance to apply to join, which will be in about a month's time."

"Excellent idea!" I said, cheering up immediately. "I've found a private flying school that can give us lessons," said

Alan. "It's the Empire Flying School at Hendon, just north of London. They'll teach us to fly for £100 each. They reckon it'll take about three weeks for us to learn. Is that all right with you?"

"Count me in!" I chuckled happily into the phone. "Hendon, here I come!"

Ten days later Alan and I reported for our first flying lessons at the Hendon school. Basically the school was little more than a field with a wooden shed in it, where the owner of the school, Mr Walter Mitchell, sat and filled out forms and answered the telephone. Our flying instructor was a Frenchman, Monsieur Chapelle. He was about 30 years old, a shortish, thin man with a big curly moustache with waxed ends. He told us that French planes were the best in the world, and that we were lucky to be learning in "one of the best creations ever seen, the Maurice Farman biplane".

Frankly, this machine looked just like a load of wood and cloth held together by a lot of wires. It was dual-control, which meant that both the instructor and the student pilot could control it. This struck me as a good idea. I'd heard that some people went up solo straight away, because there was no room for two people in some planes. It occurred me to me that it would be useful to have someone to take over if you had trouble with the controls and were a thousand feet up in the air. The biplane, which was known as a "Shorthorn", had two long wings – one above the pilot, one below – and was driven by a Renault engine. The instructor sat at the back, and the student sat at the front. Alan and I tossed a coin to see which of us would go first, and I called heads and won.

Monsieur Chapelle put on his leather cap and goggles, and climbed into the rear seat behind the pilot's. I also put on my leather cap and goggles and clambered into the seat at the front.

"Those bars, where you put your feet, are the rudder bars," explained Monsieur Chapelle. "The stick in front of you is called the joystick and that controls when you go up and when you go down. Just rest your hands and feet lightly on the controls and feel when they move. Notice how they move when I operate them.

"Do not attempt to put any pressure on them yourself, just get the feeling of what they do. I shall get us off the ground this first time. Once we are in the air, I shall pass the controls over to you. Is that clear?"

"Perfectly," I said.

The school's mechanic, a giant of a man called George, had been waiting beside the plane while Monsieur Chapelle and I got in. Now George went to the large wooden propeller at the front of the plane and took hold of it in both of his huge hands.

"Ignition off!" he bellowed.

"Ignition off!" confirmed Monsieur Chapelle in a shout from behind me.

George then began to turn the propeller slowly.

"He is priming the engine from the carburettor by turning the propeller," explained Monsieur Chapelle. "When the engine is primed, he will give it one last turn to get the engine going."

George kept turning the propeller. From the sweat pouring down his face from the effort, it looked like hard work, even for a big man like him. Finally, he stopped and called out, "Contact!"

Monsieur Chapelle switched on the ignition and echoed the cry. George gave the heavy propeller one last quarter turn. Behind me I could hear a handle being turned round quickly.

"I am turning the handle of the starter magneto to boost the spark at the plugs!" shouted Monsieur Chapelle into my ear. "The magneto is the electrical motor that makes the engine spark and burn the fuel."

Suddenly I heard the sound of the engine behind us kicking into life, and then it began to rattle with an alarming coughing and chattering sound, like a car engine with hiccups.

George stepped back swiftly from the propeller and out of the path of the plane, ducking his head down to make sure he was under the wings. And then we were moving forward.

We rolled across the grass, bumping and jerking along, getting nearer and nearer all the time to the hedge at the edge of the field ... and then suddenly we were up in the air, and flying over the hedge! It was an absolutely exhilarating feeling. We were only about eight feet off the ground, but I was flying through the air!

Keeping a light touch on the controls as Monsieur Chapelle had instructed, I felt the joystick being pulled back and we began to go up. Up, up, up. Soon the ground was far below us. From my position at the front I could see for miles. Houses and buildings were tiny. People were just specks.

"I am passing the controls to you," shouted Monsieur Chapelle from behind me. "Keep a firm grip on them. If you get into difficulty, or if I tell you to, release your hold on all the controls immediately and I will take over. Is that clear?"

"Clear, Monsieur Chapelle," I replied.

"At first, just keep the plane on the course which it is already flying," instructed Monsieur Chapelle. "Hold it steady. Use the rudders."

I felt an enormous sense of excitement as the bars responded to the pressure of my feet. That feeling of resistance that let me know that I was in control. I was flying this machine. Me, Jack Fairfax.

"You are now going to take the plane up higher," shouted Monsieur Chapelle. "But gently. Slowly pull back on the joystick."

I did as instructed. Higher we went, and higher. Now I began to feel the air getting colder, a chill wind picking at the skin on my face.

"Level off!" Monsieur Chapelle called.

I levelled the joystick and flew in a straight line for a while.

"We are now at 3,500 feet," came Monsieur Chapelle's voice from behind me. "The higher you go, the colder it is. Take us back down to 2,000 feet."

I pushed the joystick forward, but unfortunately I pushed it too hard, and we suddenly dropped into a dive. I felt the joystick pulling back in my hand and the plane levelling out, and realized that Monsieur Chapelle had momentarily retaken control of the joystick.

"Gently, mon ami!" called Monsieur Chapelle. "If you dive too fast and too steeply you can go into a spin. If you go into a spin you will not come out of it easily and the next thing you will do is crash into the ground nose first, and die. I do not recommend it."

He released the joystick and I felt the pressure of it in my grip again. This time I eased it forward much more gently, and we descended into a slower dive.

"Good!" said Monsieur Chapelle. "Level her out now!"

Down at 2,000 feet that frosty feeling on my skin eased off.

"We will now do some manoeuvres, left and right," instructed Monsieur Chapelle.

For the next ten minutes I followed his shouted instructions: turning the plane to the left, then to the right, locating and following the course of a railway line, and then a river. During this I had to admit that I had lost all sense of direction and hadn't got the faintest idea where we were. From this height the countryside looked much the same, whichever way I looked.

Finally, Monsieur Chapelle said, "We will now return to the airfield. I will navigate you to the field, but on this first occasion I will carry out the landing. As before, you will just let your hands and feet rest on the controls and feel what they do. Is that clear?"

"Clear!" I called back.

To my surprise, I discovered that we weren't far from Hendon. Monsieur Chapelle had obviously been manoeuvring me so that my left and right turns were all the time heading us back in a circle towards the flying school. We were still some miles away, but I could see the field and the wooden hut in the distance. Monsieur Chapelle instructed me, "Gently ease the joystick forward!"

I did as he ordered, and we began to go down, heading straight for the hedge that bordered the flying school field. Down, down, down, we went, until Monsieur Chapelle called out, "Level out!"

I levelled out, and Monsieur Chapelle ordered, "Release the controls to me!"

As he had instructed, I released my firm grip on them but kept my hands and feet loosely touching them, feeling their movement, the way they went up and down and moved from side to side as we flew over the hedge.

The next second the ground was rushing up towards us. There was a bump as we came down, then we lifted up again, and a second bump as we touched the ground again, and finally we were bouncing over the uneven ground, slowing down. As we coasted to a halt, I wanted to shout out loud with joy. For the very first time, I had flown!

After my lesson I sat on an old chair beside Mr Mitchell's wooden hut and watched as Monsieur Chapelle took Alan up in the Shorthorn for his first lesson. As I watched them lift off the ground and disappear into the distance, I relived the excitement of my first flight. It was a feeling like I'd never known before. It wasn't like climbing a chapel steeple or a peak in the Lake District. This was altogether different. This was being free of the ground completely.

Later that afternoon, as Alan's driver, Woodson, drove us back to Alan's place, we talked about what a completely wonderful experience it had been. Alan's place was at Radlett in Hertfordshire, which was about ten miles away from Hendon. His parents had invited me to come and stay with them while Alan and I were doing our training. It was a welcome offer and meant that I didn't have the long journey from Oxford every day, nor have to find digs locally.

"I thought Monsieur Chapelle was excellent," I said. "A damn good instructor."

"Yes," agreed Alan. "These Frenchies seem to have a talent for aeroplanes. I was talking to Mr Mitchell while you were up in the air. According to him, if it wasn't for the French there'd be no such thing as aeroplanes."

"What about the Wright Brothers?" I asked. "They were American, surely."

"Yes, but according to Mitchell they used a lot of French designs in their plane. Plus, it was the French who first used the rotary engine. In 1909, he says."

"I expect he's right," I said. "Frankly, I wouldn't know a rotary engine from a lawnmower. But then, I don't want to be a mechanic, I want to be a pilot."

When we got back to the Dixons' house I telephoned Father and told him that I had been up in a plane and had landed safely, and that everything was going well. Although I guessed that he was relieved that I hadn't killed myself and my instructor on my first flight, I detected a note of disappointment in his voice on the phone. He obviously was still hoping that I'd get over this "flying madness", as he'd put it, and join the Greys.

Every weekday for the next three weeks, Alan and I drove to Hendon for more lessons from Monsieur Chapelle. By the end of that first week we were both flying solo. Finally, on 23rd August, both Alan and I were awarded our flying certificates by the school. We were now both qualified pilots – at least as far as civilian flying was concerned. The next stage was to learn to fly military planes.

During our time at the Empire Flying School, we'd been in touch with the applications board of the Royal Flying Corps, and the day after we got our flying certificates from Mr Mitchell, Alan and I were accepted by the RFC and told to report to Farnborough.

It was with a feeling of great gratitude that I shook Monsieur Chapelle's hand as we left Hendon for the last time. He had safely taken us through every aspect of flying, and it was thanks to him that we were now both on our way to the RFC School, and eventually to the Western Front.

Alan and I spent the next month at Farnborough, carrying out more flights – some dual-control, some solo – in a variety of planes. As well as the Farman biplane, we also flew pretty ancient Caudrons, which were the devil to control in windy conditions, and Avros, which were much better to fly in my opinion.

The worst of the lot was the "Bloater". The Bloater's proper name was the BE8 and it was supposed to be an improvement on the earlier BE and BE2. Frankly, I found it to be an appalling machine. And I wasn't the only one. All the chaps had difficulty with it. It was unstable both on the ground and in the air. At the slightest touch it was prone to go into a spin, and it took all your strength and skill to get out of it. The dreadful thing had to be handled with kid gloves: too much rudder or too much bank and the thing threw itself all over the place. I suppose the reasoning behind getting us to fly these awful machines was that if we could handle a Bloater, we could handle anything.

After four weeks of this, Alan and I had both clocked up enough hours in the air and passed all our exams to qualify for our "wings" – our pilots' badges. We thought we were now ready to fly off and face the enemy, but we were in for a shock.

"Right," our flight commander, Captain Walters, told us. "You're both being posted to Upavon in Wiltshire for some advanced training."

"But, sir," I protested. "Surely we're needed at the Front, fighting the Huns. We've got our wings, after all."

"You may have got your wings, Lieutenant Fairfax," said Walters, "but the RFC needs to know that when you get out there, you won't lose us any planes. They are in short supply and we have to know you'll be able to take good care of them. So, you've got a few more weeks of very vital advanced training at the best flying school in the world. Take advantage of it. It could save your life. Some of these Huns are amazingly talented fliers, and you need to know what you're going to be up against."

And so Alan and I went off for yet more training. It was a very frustrating time for me. I was desperate to get out to France and play my part in the War. Yet here I was, with 1915 coming to an end, still stuck in England. Upavon was a dreadful place. Or maybe it was just that we were seeing it at the worst time of year, in the damp of winter. The flying school was set in the middle of Salisbury Plain and our accommodation was in wooden huts, which let in the cold and damp. However, the training we received was superb.

And not just the actual flying training, but also the lectures we were given.

We were instructed that the primary task of the Royal Flying Corps was to act as aerial observers. To report enemy positions and troop movements in order that the Top Brass could take proper decisions about battle strategy and the movements of our own troops. To that effect, we were shown how to take photographs from the air using large wooden box-cameras fixed to the side of the plane. We were also taught how to locate and identify positions on maps from the air, and how to identify enemy weapons.

As "observation and reporting of the enemy" was rated the highest priority for the Flying Corps, those of us who flew single-seater planes were told that our job was to give protection to the two-seater observer planes. The two-seaters had a pilot and an observer, who also acted as a gunner, operating the plane's machine-gun. Our job was to fly with these observer planes and defend them from attack from German aircraft. In turn, if we came upon a German two-seater observation plane, or any German plane, come to that, then we were to shoot it down. So we had to know all we could about the German aircraft, and the flying abilities of the German pilots.

We were told that the most recent German fighter planes we would be coming up against were the Fokker monoplanes, single-seater fighters with deadly accurate fixed guns. According to our instructors, early on in the War pilots had just been armed with a pistol. The only way of shooting at an enemy was to point the pistol at his plane, press the trigger and hope you hit him – which, considering the way planes juddered about all the time, going up and down in the air, was pretty unlikely.

Then someone fixed a machine-gun to the edge of the cockpit of a small plane, and the fighter plane was created. The biggest problem with this, however, was that the pilot couldn't fire the machine-gun straight ahead for fear of shooting his own propeller. The French and Germans were the first ones to come up with an answer: each invented different sorts of gears, one called an "interrupter", the other known as a "synchronizer". Both systems meant that a pilot could fire his machine-gun without his propeller being hit.

Our own side was developing new planes all the time, of course, such as the Sopwith Strutter (which was a two-seater reconnaissance machine with a synchronized Vickers gun at the front for the pilot and a Lewis machine-gun at the rear for the observer), and the Sopwith Pup (which was a single-seater version of the Strutter). But now the Germans had come up with the most fearsome advance in fighter technology yet with the Fokker E series and the Albatross monoplanes, which had accounted for many of our chaps being shot down.

"Remember, the Fokker are the best German machines, so the best German pilots make a point of taking them as soon as they appear," our instructor warned us. "The best pilots together with the best machines make a formidable combination. But they can be beaten."

To show us how they could be beaten we had instruction on tactics in air battles – and not just dry old lectures from men who'd only ever seen a plane in a picture, but gripping reports from flying aces who were actually out there fighting the Hun in the sky. They told us how to attack an enemy.

"In a battle in the sky, your biggest assets are your reflexes," one ace, Captain Harry Manners, told us. Manners was reported to have 17 kills to his name, which made him a hero in our eyes.

"Unfortunately," he continued, "reflex reactions come with practice and experience, which means you lot are going to have to make sure you stay alive long enough to develop them."

We all laughed at this, but I noticed that Manners didn't join in.

"It's very easy to get your attention stuck on something," Manners continued. "A target on the ground, say, or an enemy aircraft at a lower altitude. Because you're watching so intently you don't notice an enemy sneak up on you from behind. The first you know about it is when the bullets hit your machine. Now when that happens, just change direction. If you freeze up, even for a fraction of a second, you're a sitting target for the next burst. Move, making sure you don't fly smack into another machine, of course. Rudder, joystick, throttle forward. A steep dive, out of his gunsights. But it's all reflexes, reacting quicker than you can actually think.

"When you come up against a two-seater, remember they're heavier than you if you're in a single-seater. They can't manoeuvre as well, so you've got an advantage. However, they have one extra man who can always keep firing at you. When attacking a two-seater make your approach from below and to the rear, where the plane has got a blind spot. If you can work in pairs, so much the better. One of you comes in on a broadside attack, opening fire at a very long range. This is the decoy attacker and won't hit the target, that's not the point. The object is to distract the attention of the crew of the enemy two-seater so the real killer can come up underneath and behind.

"If you're in a single-seater attacking on your own, use the sun and clouds. Come out of the sun, so that it dazzles your opponent. If you want to hide, use a cloud as cover."

For me and Alan, the most exciting part of this training was the actual exercises. We flew in pairs, firing imaginary shells at one another and learning how to use the sun, clouds, and wind to gain a tactical advantage. We flew high in the sky, looping the loop to escape from our "opponent" who was chasing us, and then coming down behind them to get a direct line on their tail. We also practised stalling our engines in mid-air to simulate engine failure, bearing in mind the firm instruction: "In case of engine failure do not attempt to turn your machine back. Put her nose down at once and make some sort of landing ahead."

Time and time again we were told that the biggest danger to us was anti-aircraft fire, commonly called "Archie", from heavy guns on the ground.

"Learn to try to avoid flying for too long in one straight line," our instructor told us. "It will give the Hun down on the ground a chance to work out your route and get their anti-aircraft guns sighted ahead of you. You'll find yourself flying straight into flak, which is the bits of shrapnel thrown out when the shell fired by the gun explodes near you. Very nasty stuff."

"Are there any plans to issue us with parachutes, sir?" asked one of our group, Banger Wilson.

Our instructor gave Wilson a hard, disapproving look. "It is not the policy of the RFC to give people an easy way out," he said sternly. "Parachutes are only issued to observers in balloons, in case their balloon gets shot down by the enemy. They have no other way of getting down except by parachute. You men, on the other hand, have been trained to fly your machine in all circumstances."

"Yes, sir, but say our plane catches fire. There's not a lot we can do with it if that happens."

"Then your job is to aim your plane at the enemy and take as many of them with you as you can," said our instructor.

As we left the lecture hall, I went up to Banger and clapped him heartily on the shoulder.

"Well, Banger," I said. "There's your answer. Death or glory."

"I can't see why us having parachutes is such a bad thing," said Wilson. "After all, if we live it means we can get back into another plane and have another go at them."

"Ah, now you're being sensible, Banger," said Alan with a grin. "You should know by now that the Top Brass are not sensible."

Our training continued for what seemed like an eternity. Our experience of flying different planes increased. As the days turned into weeks, and the weeks turned into months, I felt that I could fly just about anything, with my particular favourites being the Vickers Gunbus and the "De Hav2", the De Havilland Scout.

Finally, at the end of February, just when I had given up hope of ever getting into the fighting before the War ended, we were told that our training was at an end. We were being sent to the Front.

Alan and I were given 48 hours' leave, and told to report back to Upavon on the Wednesday, ready to kit up and fly out to France on the Friday with the rest of our group, 32 Squadron.

We didn't want to waste any precious time telephoning our respective homes and arranging for cars to come and collect us. Instead we found a driver who was returning to London after delivering a load of supplies to the airfield, and gave him a pound to make a couple of detours on his way back: dropping me off at Bowness Hall, and Alan at Radlett. It was money well spent.

Both Mother and Nanna made admiring noises about my uniform, and the wings I was proudly displaying, but I could tell that Father was disappointed. For him, it was the wrong uniform. I should have been wearing the colours of the Royal Scots Dragoon Guards, the Greys. But he didn't dwell on the topic.

"Congratulations on getting your wings, Jack," he said. "But, if it doesn't go as you planned, remember your promise. You will always find a commission in the Greys."

"Absolutely, Father," I said.

Inwardly I thought to myself, the only way this won't go as I planned is if I get shot down. And if that happens I don't think there'll be much left of me.

I spent time with Nanna, telling her about my flying experiences, but I could see, despite her expressions of being interested, that all the technical talk was beyond her. Finally she smiled, patted me on the knee, and said, "Jack, I know you find all this mechanical talk about rudders and joysticks absolutely fascinating, but you have to remember that I am an old woman. When I was a girl, the motorcar hadn't even been invented, let alone the aeroplane. I love to hear you talk about it, but it's all gibberish to me. The horse and carriage were our means of transport. Ships used sails, not engines."

I was also able to catch up on how Oswald was doing. During his time at the Front he'd come home on leave to England only once, a couple of months earlier, just after Christmas.

"I wish you'd been able to get home too, at that same time, Jack," my mother said. "It would have been nice to have had both my boys home together."

"But I was in training, Mother," I pointed out.

"There has to be a special reason for getting leave."

"Jack's right," said my father, backing me up. "Even if it is the Flying Corps, military rules still apply. You know that, Elspeth. Remember how rarely I used to be able to make it home when I was in the Greys."

"Yes, but you were in Africa," countered Mother.

"Jack was just in Salisbury."

"Rules are rules, Mother," I said. "Anyway, how was Oswald?"

"He seems to be getting on quite well," said Mother.

"He's getting on very well," interrupted Father.

"You know he's a captain. Well, if he carries on the way he is, I'm sure he can go as high in the Regiment as he wishes. It wouldn't surprise me to see him being made a major before very long. He's as able on the Front as he was at school. Oswald is a natural commander."

The implication being that I wasn't. I didn't argue. If that was Father's opinion, then I was happy to let him go on thinking it. At least, until the time when I came back from the Front as a flying ace, laden with medals. Then we'd see what he said about me.

I fixed up for Alan's driver to collect me on his way to the airbase at Upavon. It made sense for us to return together, especially as Alan's car would almost have to pass our front door.

"How were your folks?" I asked.

"Pretty cheerful," replied Alan. "Yours?"

I gave a wry grin. "I still get the impression from my father that I'm the black sheep of the family," I said. "Because you didn't go into the Greys?"

I nodded. "He thinks this flying business is just a fad,"

I said. "His attitude makes me even more determined to prove him wrong. I'm going to go up and shoot down so many German planes that the War Office will give me a letter saying I've virtually won this war on my own! We'll see if he's still got this same pig-headed opinion when I show him that."

Alan laughed. "Poor old Jack," he said. "I'm glad I don't have the same family traditions to live up to."

We arrived at Upavon to find the place in a frenzy of activity. We had barely stepped out of our car when Major Govan, our flight commander, hurried up to us. "Fairfax! Dixon!" he called. "Get over to the field and get your machines sorted out. You've both drawn a De Havilland and they'll need rigging if we're to leave on time tomorrow, so jump to it."

"Yes, sir!" we chorused.

We turned to each other in delight.

"A De Hav each!" Alan chortled.

We'd both been hoping that we'd get a De Hav. The Vickers was an excellent machine, but both Alan and I considered the De Havilland to be the crème de la crème of fighter aircraft.

We hurried to our quarters just to dump our bags on our bunks and then dashed to the field, as we had been ordered, where we found our machines waiting for us.

All pilots in the RFC were given a fitter and rigger to help them fix up their machines, but it was up to the individual pilot to make sure the plane was in proper order. This made sense because a plane that wasn't in top condition could be a death trap to the pilot. Rigging meant adjusting the wires that held the wings in place on a biplane. You had to make sure the tension of the wires was just right so that the plane could carry out its manoeuvres properly, without the wings collapsing.

Our squadron spent the rest of that day preparing our machines and loading our possessions into the transport, which was setting off for France before us to establish a base for our arrival.

At 1100 hours on Friday, the 16 planes of 32 Squadron assembled on the field ready for take-off in lines of four. Each line is known as a "flight" and Alan, Banger Wilson, Monty Johnson and I were in the third flight. At the signal, we all started our engines up at the same time, and then the first four planes of first flight set off, rolling together over the green grass of the field, then rising up into the air. They were followed by the second flight, then my group in the third flight, with the fourth flight following behind us.

The first flight had been circling over the Wiltshire plain, holding position while the other flights got off the ground, and now, finally with all 16 planes in the air, we grouped and headed towards our first point of call – Folkestone on the Kent coast.

It was a glorious feeling flying together in formation. The

sky was clear and blue. No cloud, no fog, no wind, perfect visibility, perfect flying weather. We all touched down safely at the airfield in Folkestone in the same sequence as before. Then we pilots went into Folkestone town for lunch at the Metropole, while the engineers refuelled and made a last check of our planes before the last leg of our journey.

Lunch was excellent. Mind, we were so full of expectation and delight that we were finally going into action, that even if we'd been served mashed potatoes and gravy, we'd have sworn it was the best meal we'd ever tasted.

After lunch, it was back to the airfield for a final check on our machines, and then the 16 of us set off across the Channel for France. We were finally going to war.

I had only flown over land before, and I have to admit that I felt intimidated by the knowledge that beneath me there was only a vast expanse of water. If I came down in that, no one would be able to come to my assistance. But I'd been a good swimmer at school, I reflected, so I could always kick off my boots and swim for shore!

Once we'd left the Channel behind us and passed over the French coast I began wondering if we'd meet a Hun, or a squadron of Hun aircraft. But there was never a real chance of that. We were still a long way behind our own front line and, according to our experts, the Germans only made exploratory raids just a few miles into enemy territory.

We flew across the French countryside for about another

hour, and landed on an airfield at a place called St Omer, which was about 20 miles behind our own front line. Even though we were a long way from the actual fighting, there was a huge military presence in the town. Military vehicles, and men in brown and blue uniforms, all hurrying to and fro as if on urgent errands. There was all the activity of war, but none of the actual battle, although we could hear the distant sound of guns firing at the Front.

All this activity wasn't confined to the airfield, but extended to the centre of St Omer itself, where we were billeted for our first night at what we were told was "the top hotel in town". The streets were filled with military vehicles and military personnel. It seemed to be a staging post for troops moving to and from the Front. The idle thought struck me that Oswald might have passed through here on his way to the Front, and I wondered if I might actually run into him.

The "top hotel" that we stayed in that night was awful. If this was the best hotel in town, I'd have hated to have stayed in the worst. We were three to a room: me, Alan and Banger sharing. The beds were comfortable enough, but the place was filthy. To have a wash meant getting water from a pump in the yard at the back of the hotel and filling a washbasin. We had been better off in our draughty wooden huts at Upavon.

Once we'd reported to the airfield the next morning and

were given our orders for the day, I soon forgot about the living conditions. Four of us – me, Alan, Banger and Monty Johnson – were to fly due west to the Front in support of an observation plane, which was going to make a reconnaissance of enemy positions.

"Remember that the observation plane is the most important machine out of all of you," our new commanding officer, Major Sanders, told us. "The observer will be bringing back photographs of the enemy positions, details of weapons and troop movements. Your job is to protect the observer plane from enemy attack at all costs. If the enemy should appear, the observer plane has orders to turn and head for the safety of our own lines. You will do your best to keep the enemy from attacking it."

I felt a huge sense of excitement and anticipation as we took off on our mission. At long last I was going to see the Western Front: the heartland of where the War was actually taking place.

We left St Omer and began our journey west, climbing to 9,000 feet. Our flight path took us over the border between France and Belgium towards Ypres. We flew in a "five of spades" formation: myself and Alan at the front, Banger and Monty flying behind us, and the two-seater observation plane in the middle.

We'd travelled for about five miles when I began to make out the very different landscape ahead of us. "Very different" was an understatement. It was like nothing I had ever seen before. As far as I could see, for 20, 30, possibly 40 miles, there was not one touch of green. Not a blade of grass, not a tree, not a bush. Just a mass of grey sludge, torn and chewed up as if a giant tractor had come in and ploughed it, throwing bits of land willy-nilly.

I looked across at the pilot of the observation plane, who pointed downwards, and then took his plane down to 5,000 feet, and then to 2,000 feet. I followed him. Now I was closer I could see the trenches carved out of the grey mud. Deep, long, pitted holes running for miles, in all directions, with other trenches joining them, like a series of sunken roads. The land on top of the trenches consisted of more mud, but with rolls of barbed wire strung out across it, again for mile after mile after mile.

I had expected to find lots of shooting and explosions, but apart from the sound of the De Hav's engine the scene was strangely silent. No guns were firing. No explosions. No rifles shooting.

I looked behind me and saw that Alan had followed me down while Banger and Monty kept at about 8,000 feet.

We followed a flight path north along our front line, identified by the khaki uniforms of the men moving below us, then we turned right and headed into German territory.

As I flew I heard the sound of rifle shots coming from just ahead and below, and realized the Germans were firing at us from their trenches. I gestured upwards, and Alan followed me back up to 8,000 feet, followed by the observation plane, where we levelled out.

I was just making a turn to head back to our own lines when, out of the corner of my eye, I caught a movement in the sky about a mile away. I turned my head and saw a pack of planes heading towards us, flying in a V-shaped formation – one plane at the front, with what looked like another half a dozen planes spreading out behind it. The Huns were on to us, and we were outnumbered!

Following orders, the observer plane immediately turned to follow a course back to our own lines.While Monty and Banger turned and followed our observer plane, Alan and I went on the offensive, heading straight towards the oncoming German planes, opening up with our guns as we did so. We were too far away to actually hit any of the enemy planes, but our shooting had the desired effect, which was to disrupt their formation.The German planes scattered left and right.

From stories we had heard from other more experienced fighter pilots, we'd been told that in a situation like this the enemy would do one of three things: turn on us; ignore us and head after our observer plane; or send half of their squadron after our observer plane while the rest ganged up on us.

We didn't wait for them to make up their minds. Alan

and I had already decided on our course of action if such an event occurred. As the seven German aircraft scattered from our flight path, we began a steep turn, me flying upwards, Alan flying down. This turn automatically brought us behind the German planes – me above them, Alan below.

The Germans had decided on a "half and half" strategy. Three of their planes had already begun their turns to chase after Alan and me, but our sudden turns had caught them on the hop. Alan came up fast, guns firing, and I zoomed down towards the nearest German fighter, my hand tight on the trigger, my gun blazing. I was lucky, I had caught my target plane halfway through his turn so he hadn't had time to get me in his gunsight. If it had been a two-seater, it would have nailed me with a burst from its swing-gun, but as a solo fighter on its own, this plane didn't have that luxury.

The constant stream of bullets from my gun raked along the fuselage of the German plane, tearing into it from front to rear. Then the plane began to head down in a spin, spiralling out of control. I levelled out from my dive, eyes darting left and right to see where the other German planes were, and where Alan was.

Alan had also caught his target napping with the swiftness of his turn, because I saw a second German plane spinning down to the ground below, this one enveloped in a cloud of black smoke. I saw flames licking at the side of the plane through the smoke, and then it vanished from my sight.

Alan was now higher than me and he brought his plane down towards me, waggling his wings slightly as he did so in a victory wiggle. He passed beneath me, and we gave each other a thumbs up. Our first victories!

But the third German plane that had set out to attack us had turned again, and was now joining the rest of its squadron coming after Monty, Banger and our observer plane. Remembering our orders, that the observer plane had to be protected at all costs, Alan and I gave chase. I made the engine give all it had, determined to catch the Germans.

Ahead of us, Monty and Banger were diving and weaving in the sky behind the observer plane, criss-crossing in front of the oncoming German fighters. Monty would make a sudden turn and lunge at the German planes, firing all the time, causing them to scatter. Then he'd loop past and head back after them again. The Germans, in their turn, were showing that they were no novices at this game. Two would soar up into the sky, and then suddenly dive down, guns blazing at our aircraft, coming at us from a blind spot.

Meanwhile the observer plane at the front droned on, nearing our own lines all the time.

Alan and I were getting closer to the Germans, and I let off a burst of gunfire into the tail of one of them. I thought I'd got him, but he lifted up and went higher. I levelled him in my gunsight again, but just as I pressed the trigger he dropped like a stone and my tracer of bullets whistled harmlessly over him.

The next second he was flying beneath me, heading back the way we'd come. I guessed he was trying to come up from behind and attack me the same way I'd just attacked him. I gave the rudder a hard turn and moved sharply to the right, and then straightened my course to get in line with Banger and Monty. I was aware that Alan was now above me. All the time there was the sound of gunfire as the Germans let off burst after burst at our planes, and we replied with our own hail of bullets.

Suddenly I saw Banger's plane drop, and then start to spin wildly. Whether Banger had been hit or whether he'd just lost control, I didn't know, I just knew that his plane was spinning, spinning, spinning, heading down towards the ground.

Angry at the German who'd done this, but not knowing which one had, I started firing wildly at the enemy aircraft, letting off long bursts. But suddenly all of the German aircraft dropped out of the sky as if at a given signal. I found myself catching up with Monty, with Alan now coming down to join me. I turned my De Hav, expecting the Germans to be pulling the same trick as before of letting us get in front of them so they could shoot us from behind, but they were all heading away, back towards their own lines. My first air battle was over.

The feelings of exhilaration that I had had my first encounter with the Germans, and had not only survived but had shot one down, were tempered with feelings of loss over Banger. Actually, if I had to admit it, it wasn't really loss that I felt. Banger was a chum from the squadron, but he and I had never been that close. My overwhelming feeling was one of relief. I couldn't help thinking that could have been me, spinning down out of the sky to my death.

That evening in the mess, Alan and I refought the air battle we'd just been involved in using cutlery and tin mugs to mark our positions, and the positions of the German planes. We never mentioned Banger, except when Alan said once, "Pity about poor old Banger," and I replied, "Yes. He was a good chap."

I found it difficult to get to sleep that night. I looked across at the empty bed where, just that morning, Banger had woken up, yawned, and complained about the dampness. He would never complain about the dampness again.

The next morning Alan and I were woken up by our batman (our servant), a man called Clark, banging on the door of our room while it was still pitch dark outside. "Major Sanders' compliments, sirs," he announced as he clattered into the room, his boots making a loud noise on the creaky wooden floorboards. "You're both on dawn patrol. So here's your cocoa and biscuits to set you up for it."

He set down the tray on the table and brought me a mug of steaming hot cocoa. I sipped it, and it was delicious. It was a long way from the hot breakfasts of eggs, salmon, mushrooms, kippers, and all the other delicacies I'd imagined I'd be eating once I'd left school, but it hit the spot.

Alan and I reached the airfield and found that Monty was already there.

"Morning, chaps!" he greeted us. "Once more into the breach, eh!"

"How can you be so cheerful at this time of day, Monty?" I complained. "It's five o'clock in the morning."

"Best time of day – that's what my father says," replied Monty breezily. "Just before dawn, before the birds start stirring. It's the best time of day for good shooting."

"Let's hope the Hun don't share his opinion," said Alan.

Our mission was to protect another two-seater observation flight. This time six of us were going up: me, Alan, Monty, Reggie, Oofy and Bingo. All good chaps, as were the two in the observer plane, brothers called Walter and Ian Wilson. Both of them were very able pilots, and they took turns to act as pilot and observer. Today, Walter was in the pilot's cockpit and Ian was taking observations.

The first streaks of light were appearing in the sky as we took off. Below, the ground was still dark, which was a mixed blessing. Although it gave us protection against any enemy aircraft flying above us, because they wouldn't be able to make us out against the darkness of the land below, it meant that we couldn't spot any enemy aircraft flying below us either.

As we rose higher and higher, anti-aircraft fire began to open up from the German lines. Explosions of red flames appeared below us as the guns on the ground went off, firing the missiles high into the air. BANG!!!! The damned things exploded in mid-air, scattering debris all around.

The smell of the German Archie was foul, mainly I guessed from the black cordite explosive the Hun used. At least it told us that it was the enemy shooting at us and not our own side, as the British and French anti-aircraft shells gave off a white smoke.

We flew in a different formation this time, me and Alan at the front, Monty and Reggie protecting the rear, and Oofy and Bingo flying on either side of the observer plane. Our orders were to fly due west to the front line, cross it, then turn left and fly north for ten miles, weaving backwards and forwards all the time to enable the Wilson brothers to take photographs and plot the German defences. Then we were to turn back and head for home.

We kept to a height of 10,000 feet to lessen the chances of being hit by the German Archie, except when the Wilson brothers decided they needed to go down lower for closer observation. We followed, keeping our eyes peeled all the time for any attacking enemy aircraft, as well as doing our best to dodge debris and missile fragments from the shells exploding around us in the sky.

We were about halfway through our mission when I was

aware of Alan suddenly breaking away from the formation and dropping down to a lower altitude. He must have spotted incoming Germans. Immediately I turned my plane in the same direction and followed him.

There they were, a formation of about eight German planes, coming at us from due east, flying out of the rising sun.

Out of the corner of my eye I saw the Wilson brothers' two-seater continue its flight north. Although common sense told them to head back across into our own territory, Ian and Walter obviously felt they hadn't achieved as much on this mission as they should have. I saw Ian in the rear observer's seat working at the big wooden box camera on the side of their plane, and then I turned my attention back to the oncoming German fighter planes.

They were nearly on us now. Alan came at them from below, his guns firing, but the German planes banked and turned and twisted in the air, and his tracer of bullets went past them. Oofy and Bingo joined me as we hurtled forward after Alan's De Hav, leaving Monty and Reggie to circle round and round the Wilson brothers' plane, protecting it as they continued their northward journey. The camera clicked and the heavy photographic plates were being changed the whole time, despite the hail of gunfire going on around them.

I picked out one of the German planes nearest to me and headed straight for it. I came in from the side, guns firing just ahead of him to hit him in the engine at the front of his plane. The Hun had seen me coming because he dropped into a steep dive to get out of the way of my bullets, and then turned up again sharply. I followed him, first down, then up, keeping a watch in all other directions as best as I could, in case I was attacked by one of the rest of the enemy squadron.

The German was good. He ducked and dived in the air, and then circled fast, and suddenly he was coming straight at me from my right-hand side, his guns chatter chattering. Luckily for me I'd got the measure of my machine and I throttled back at the apex of my turn, allowing the De Hav to side-slip for just a few seconds, but long enough to take me out of the German's gunsights so I could put it into a dive.

Down I went, and now in daylight I could see the ground below – the trenches, the destruction, the mud and the mass of men – for as far as the eye could see. But only for a second, because then I banked and put the De Hav into a turn, bringing it under my German opponent. He tried to turn sharply, too, but the movement was too fast for him and his plane juddered. It was only for a second, but it was all I needed. As he recovered and began to turn away, I let him have a burst of gunfire straight into the tail of his plane, tearing it to shreds.

Without controls, the German's plane gave a sickening lurch, and then plummeted out of the sky, heading towards the ground 10,000 feet below. Meanwhile the rest of the air battle was continuing. I could see that Alan was still active, his De Hav zooming in and out between the enemy aircraft, guns firing all the time. Reggie and Bingo were also in the thick of it. It was madness up there, planes hurtling left and right, looping and turning, tracers of gunfire tearing through the sky. There was no sign of Monty's plane. Oofy was shadowing the Wilson brothers' plane, and as I glimpsed in their direction I saw the brothers' plane turn and head for our own lines. Ian must have got as many photographs of the enemy as he needed. Now I could only see six German planes in the air. As Oofy escorted the Wilsons in their observer plane over the line towards our own side, Alan, Reggie, Bingo and I gave one last flurry of gunfire at the German planes, then turned and flew after Oofy and the Wilsons.

The Germans also decided they'd had enough.

They'd chased us back to our own side of the line, so they turned and headed back to the safety of their own positions.

As I flew back with the rest of our formation towards our airfield base, I wondered what had happened to Monty. Had he been shot down? Had his plane been hit? Had he been forced to land? One thing was sure as we returned: another of us was missing.

Over the next few days I kept my ears open for any news of Monty, but there was no word. None of us had seen his plane go down, but then we'd been too busy carrying on with our own battles in the sky. Reggie thought he'd seen one of the Germans fire a burst straight at Monty, but he couldn't be sure. And so Alistair Montgomery, aged 18, went on the list as "Missing, presumed dead".

After those first two days of air battles, in which we lost Banger and then Monty, the days became a sort of blur. Each day we went up into the air, and on most occasions we encountered German fighters. Every time we came home with yet another of our pilots gone.

By some miracle Alan and I survived, coming back from mission after mission. Now and again when we landed we found our fuselage was torn and riddled with bullets, but we arrived back safely, another day older – another day alive.

Once in a while the weather was too bad for us to go up, with thick clouds forming, and on those days I was glad of the respite. It was a chance to unwind just a bit, to ease the tension that came from going up into the air, knowing that each time it could be your last hour alive.

Over the next few months, familiar faces disappeared and were replaced by new, shining young faces. Many of them, lacking the experience of us old hands who'd been battling Germans in the air for a couple of months, didn't last longer than a couple of days.

Sometimes, seeing one of the new chaps setting off, bouncing across the airfield in a way that showed he was still coming to terms with his machine, I gave thanks for all the advanced training at Upavon. At the time I'd resented the hours I'd spent there, keeping me from the Front, but now I saw that those few extra weeks of hard and repetitive training had helped to keep me alive.

Meanwhile, for the troops on the ground, the War dragged on, with the front line moving a few hundred yards one way, then a few hundred yards back. Despite the dangers we encountered every time we went up, our life in the Royal Flying Corps seemed like luxury when we heard reports about what was happening in the trenches. The Battle of Verdun had been going on since February. Six weeks later neither side had gained any ground, but there were reports that a million men had died in that battle alone. A million. It made our losses seem paltry.

I wondered how Oswald was doing. Was he even alive? Information seemed harder and harder to come by, with any questions being met with a stern look and the reply that "the enemy may have spies listening".

And so, ignorant of what was happening in the wider war, as well as not knowing which side was winning, we continued to go up and fight the enemy.

MID-JUNE 1916

It was some time in June that Alan and I, and a whole load of new chaps, were sent off on yet another flight, protecting an observation plane. I can't even remember the purpose of this particular mission. Each one had started to blur one into another. Every time we flew over a sea of mud and barbed wire, carved with deep trenches and huge craters where bombs had ripped the earth, sometimes 20 feet deep.

We were under attack from a group of German fighters – about six Fokkers. Only these were different from the usual German planes. Instead of the regular dull brown colour with black crosses painted on the wing, these were painted bright yellow, and one of them even had a huge grinning face painted on the propeller mounting at the front. It gave me a bit of a shock when I saw them. For a moment I wasn't even sure if they were fighter planes or if it was some kind of flying carnival. And then they opened fire.

As before, we took initial evasive action to get away from their line of fire, though at the same time making sure that the observer plane we were protecting was covered. Today it was my turn to take the rearguard position and oversee the safety of the observer plane. The problem with the two-seater planes was that they were slower than any single-seater, because of the extra weight and so more vulnerable to attack. However, the observer did have a mounted machine-gun able to move in different directions. It could shoot at planes attacking from above, the rear, or from the sides.

The yellow plane with the grinning face came hurtling out of the pack straight for our observer plane, guns blazing, obviously intent on a quick kill. Our observer plane dropped down, the observer firing upwards aiming to catch the yellow plane in its forward trajectory, while I came in fast from the left. Between the two of us I expected we would down this brightly coloured monstrosity within seconds, but just as I thought I had a sure line of fire the German pilot banked sharply and my line of tracer missed him.

The German pilot had banked so sharply that I was sure he had gone into the turn too fast and was going to go into a spin, but, to my shock, he continued the sharp turn, doubling back on himself, and I suddenly found him sharp on my right. The next second there was a RAT-A-TAT of exploding gunfire and my engine cut out, the propeller juddering to a halt. He had shot clean through my engine.

My plane began to fall out of the sky and I went into reflex action, remembering the many times I'd practised "what to do in the event of engine failure". Only this was not just a failed engine, this was a dead engine. And I was

10,000 feet above the ground in a machine that was suddenly heavier than the air I was flying in. I was fighting a losing battle against gravity. And then an even bigger horror struck me as I began to feel a stinging wetness on my clothes and on my face. The German's bullets had cut through my fuel line and I was being sprayed with gasoline. It was every pilot's nightmare, to be trapped in a burning plane.

First rule: Don't panic.

Second rule: Put the nose of the plane down and use air currents to keep the plane as level as possible while gravity takes hold – which meant, keep going forward. But in the sudden movement of action, I'd lost my sense of direction. I didn't know whether I was heading towards our own lines, or the German positions.

Third rule: Look ahead for a flat area, such as a field, to land in. My problem was that, as far as I could see, there was no flat land, it was all mud and trenches and barbed wire. Any fields were miles away from the Front. The gasoline kept spraying out and now my clothes were soaked with it. Please, don't let it catch fire, I prayed silently.

My engine was off, which was a good thing. It only needed one spark and I knew I'd go up in a ball of flames. The danger was now my propeller. The fuel tank was at the front of the plane, close behind the propeller, so if the propeller started up and fired the magneto, the force of air generated by it would fan the flames straight at me.

Although the propeller had stopped after the engine failed, and seemed to be stuck in one position, I could see it wobbling slightly. Feverishly I hoped that the propeller had jammed. If it was still free, then it could start rotating of its on accord in the wind. As the propeller was locked in direct drive to the magneto of the engine, if the propeller began to turn, then the magneto would also turn, which would produce sparks. Then my only hope was that the magneto had also been shattered, or was jammed solid.

During all the time I was thinking this I was coming down ... down ... down ... trying my hardest to hold the plane level as the wind buffeted the wings and body.

"Glide!" I yelled aloud at the plane, heaving back on the joystick to stop the nose of my plane from going too far down, but not too hard because that could send the plane into a spin.

Down, down I went... The ground below and in front of me was clearer now, coming up fast. So far the propeller hadn't moved. My luck was still holding. Then, to my horror, I saw the propeller shift slightly, and begin to turn.

"NO!" I yelled aloud, and waited for the sudden WHOOF of sparks from the magneto igniting the gasoline and the flames. But instead the plane just continued its descent, getting faster now as it neared the ground. The German's bullets must have smashed the magneto. At least, I hoped so. I tensed, waiting for any sound of sparks or small explosions that might signify fire. I was still too high to leap out of the plane and survive, but I'd rather die from falling than be burnt to death.

Down and down I came, and now I was aware that the trenches and the barbed wire and the mud were getting nearer and nearer ... men were shouting, shouts of anger and alarm, but no one was shooting at me. I was coming down behind our own lines. Providing the magneto didn't suddenly kick into life, all I had to do was hold the plane level and hope it didn't fall apart as we hit the ground. With nowhere to land properly, it meant just bringing it down where I could.

Suddenly everything was flashing up at me and hurtling past at incredible speed – barbed wire, wooden posts, banks of mud. There was a sickening crunch as my undercarriage hit something, then my left wing smashed into something else and just collapsed, the rigging fell apart, and the whole plane began to leap up into the air, and then roll.

I held on to the controls as tightly as I could, but then the plane gave a last massive jerk and I found the controls coming away in my hand. I was flying through the air, head over heels, when suddenly I hit a pool of water and began to sink.

As the thick, foul-smelling water closed over my head, the thought went through my mind: Oh God, I survived the fall and now I'm going to drown. I pushed myself up to the surface of the water and struck out for a wall of mud at one side. My hair and eyes were so wet with sludge that I could barely see. My hands touched the wall of mud, then my feet found some kind of footing beneath the water and I began to push myself up.

"Here you are, mate!" called a voice. "I'll give you a hand!"

A soldier had appeared at the top, and held out his hand to me. I grasped it, and he hauled me upwards, out of the way. I flopped over the top and rolled down the other side into more mud.

"Are you hurt?" asked the soldier, who sounded like a Cockney.

"I don't know yet," I said. "I haven't had time to find out."

This made the soldier laugh out loud.

"Here, mates!" he called out. "This bloke don't know if he's hurt. Says he hasn't had a chance to find out yet." At this there was even more laughter. It hadn't sounded that funny to me when I'd said it, but I suppose these chaps in the trenches didn't get much to laugh at. I struggled to get out of the mud I was stuck in and push myself upright, but as I did so I felt a terrific pain shoot up my leg from my ankle, and I fell over. "Ow!" I exclaimed. "I think I've broken my ankle."

In fact, as I discovered when they took me to the nearest casualty station, I hadn't broken my ankle, merely sprained it. This seemed to annoy the doctor on duty very much.

"Do you realize I have men coming in here with serious injuries!" he raged at me as I lay on the bed in the station.

"Men who are dying. Men with limbs that need amputating. Men who are blinded. Men with holes in their stomachs that their guts poke out of, and you dare to come in here with a sprained ankle!"

"It wasn't my fault!" I protested, pretty annoyed myself. "I didn't know it was just a sprain. It hurt very much and I thought it was broken. Next time I'll ask the Germans to make sure they injure me properly before I'm brought in."

But the doctor had decided I wasn't worth arguing with and he just gave a nurse instructions to bandage my ankle and then kick me out.

Actually, I had to admit, looking round that casualty station, I felt every sympathy with him for his attitude. It was exactly as he had said, there were all manner of injuries there. Some of them were so bad that I couldn't imagine how the poor people suffering from them could survive. Then I reflected that many of them wouldn't, many of them would be dead by the morning.

Seeing the War at close quarters was a shock. I'd seen injured men, I'd seen dead men, but it was the conditions that everyone was living and working and fighting in that shocked me.

I'd also seen the mud before, but the closest I'd been was 500 feet above it. Here at ground level, the mud dominated everything. It was grey and it stank, the putrid smell filling my nostrils. It made me want to heave. But maybe it was the stench of death, not just the mud, because wherever you looked there were the remains of rotting corpses. Many of them lay out in the area called no-man's-land, which was the patch of ground between our front-line trenches and those of the Germans. No-man's-land was a tangle of rows and rows of barbed wire, aimed at preventing a sudden attack by either side, and bits of bodies and all manner of other things still hung caught on the wire.

After looking at the conditions in the trenches, I felt guilty about complaining about our quarters back at St Omer. By comparison, we were living in luxury. Again, I thought of Oswald and wondered how he was coping.

I asked one of the telegraph operators at the casualty station to wire a message to my unit, telling them that I was safe and well (except for a sprained ankle) and would be returning for action as soon as I could get there.

Fortunately for me, a truck was leaving from the casualty station and going in the general direction of St Omer. After a series of three lifts – one on the truck, one in a battered old car, and the final part on the back of a motorcycle – I arrived back at our base two days later.

The first person I saw as I limped back into the operations hut on the airfield at St Omer was Alan, who let out a yell of joy when he saw me, and then, as he saw me limping, burst into laughter.

"That's a fine welcome back!" I complained. "What's so funny?"

"A sprained ankle!" Alan laughed. "You're shot down from 10,000 feet..."

"Not that high," I said. "Anyway, I was able to glide down."

"Your plane breaks up into pieces, and you're stuck in the middle of a ground battle between our boys and the Hun, shot and shell all around you, and all you come out of it with is a sprained ankle!"

He laughed again. "By heavens, Jack, everyone should have your luck. Lucky Jack Fairfax I'm going to call you from now on."

"I'd rather you didn't," I said. "It might be rather tempting fate."

"What I want to know is how you got out of it," put in Reggie, who came over to join us. "So I know what to do if it ever happens to me."

"The first thing to do is be shot by a gentleman," I said. "One who shoots your engine and doesn't follow it up shooting you when you're on your way down, like some of the swine. Who was he, anyway? Does anyone know? Swanning around the skies in that flying banana, someone has to know who he is."

"His name's Otto Von Klempter," replied Alan.

"But why on earth paint his plane that dreadful colour?" I asked. "And that silly face painted on his propeller mounting. It's almost as if he wants to draw attention to himself."

"He does," said Reggie. "Did you notice that all six planes were painted the same yellow? It's like having team colours. Von Klempter is their leader, so he had the face painted on his propeller mounting so that everyone will know when they've been hit by him and his team."

"What arrogance!" I snorted.

"It's more than arrogance," said Alan, "it's part of a major offensive on the part of the Hun. Those six yellow planes you saw were just the start. The day after you came down, there were fourteen of them in the sky, all painted the same yellow colour. And other groups of German flyers are doing the same, all in groups of fourteen. They're called Jastas."

"Well I call them idiots," I said. "You can paint your plane all colours of the rainbow, it doesn't make you a better flyer."

"But Von Klempter got you, Jack," Reggie pointed out. "Which makes him a pretty crack shot."

"Yes, all right, he can fly," I admitted grudgingly. "But he caught me by surprise. Next time, I'll be ready for him. Wait and see what happens tomorrow."

However the next day there was to be no flying for me. At least, not in combat.

"We're running low on machines, Lieutenant Fairfax," Major Sanders told me when I reported to him for duty. "There's a two-seater going to Farnborough tomorrow.

You're to go with the pilot and pick up a new machine, and then bring it back. Think you can do that without smashing this one up?"

I ignored his sarcastic comment and saluted smartly. "Absolutely, Major," I said.

So the next day I said goodbye to Alan, Reggie and the rest of the chaps, and took the observer's seat in an old BE2C, and we set off back to England.

As we flew over the Channel I reflected about the last time I'd flown over this particular stretch of water, and how much I'd changed in so short a time. A few months ago, I'd been an eager young pilot, keen to get to grips with the Hun. I was now just four months older, but I felt years older in experience. I'd lost so many colleagues it was difficult to remember them all. You shook a young man by the hand to welcome him one day then, a day or so later, he was gone. It was even hard to remember what their names were or what they looked like. Sometimes it seemed a miracle that Alan and I were still alive.

LATE JUNE 1916

When we arrived at Farnborough I found that the plane I was due to pick up had been destroyed by a trainee pilot the day before.

"It's going to be a couple of days before the replacement arrives," the base commander informed me. "You must be due for some leave. Why don't you take a 48-hour pass. Go up to London, see some of the sights, get the War out of your system for a bit."

His suggestion seemed a very civilized idea to me, with one difference. After the chaos of the War, and the constant daily aerial combat, 48 hours of peace and quiet seemed a better prospect than the noise of London. I thought I'd take the opportunity to nip home to Bowness Hall and proudly show Father and Mother that their flyer son was in action, with a couple of victories to his credit, and a war injury – even if it was only a sprained ankle. I was also curious to find out if there was any news of Oswald.

I telephoned from Farnborough and advised Guest, our butler, that I was on my way home for a short visit, and would be with the family as soon as I'd sorted out the necessary trains.

It was about half past seven in the evening when the taxi dropped me off at the entrance to the Hall, and I limped up the steps. I have to confess that I possibly overdid the limp, just to add a touch of glamour to the image of the Flying Fighter-Pilot War Hero Returning Home.

I don't know if I expected a very warm welcome, but I didn't get one. Mother and Father weren't the most demonstrative of people at the best of times, their motto being: "Showing your feelings can be interpreted as a sign of weakness." So I received a slightly distant hug from my mother, and a formal handshake from my father.

"You're limping," my mother commented.

"Yes," I said. "But it's just a slight scratch. I was shot down, but luckily I wasn't really harmed, so I'll be able to get back in action as soon as I return to France."

I felt a bit of a cheat as I said it, so I added truthfully, "Actually, I just sprained my ankle."

Unlike Alan, neither of them laughed. Mother nodded absently and said, "You were obviously lucky."

"Dinner is ready," Father announced. "We thought you might be hungry after your journey, so we told Cook to prepare it for as soon as you arrived. Is that all right with you?"

"Unless you want to freshen up first?" suggested Mother.

"No, no," I assured them. "Food first. Believe me, after the rations I've lived on for the past months, my idea of heaven is a meal cooked by Mrs Gussett."

I expected my father to make some sort of rejoinder, like telling me how, in the Boer War, he and his troops were forced to live on hard biscuits and rainwater, but instead he just nodded and said, "I am sure Mrs Gussett will have done you proud."

As we walked into the dining room, I thought that it was a strange sort of homecoming. Cheerless, even a sense of disappointment. I wondered if Father was still upset over the fact that I'd joined the RFC instead of the Regiment. We sat down to dinner, just the three of us. Nanna was dining in her rooms. The meal was superb. Mrs Gussett had excelled herself. Or maybe it was just that I'd been eating military rations for so long that I'd forgotten what good home-cooked food tasted like. As we ate, I talked about the War, and what life was like in the Flying Corps.

"Very different, I expect, to what poor Oswald's experiencing there. I've seen it up close and frankly I can't see how anyone can survive in it. It's just mud and barbed wire and trenches for as far as the eye can see," I chuckled. "Not at all the sort of thing that Oswald's used to. Remember how he never liked getting his shoes dirty? Well he'll be getting them dirty out there, sure enough."

There was a strange, strangled sound from my mother,

which caused me to look up from my plate. My mother had her table napkin to her face, and I realized she was dabbing at her eyes. I noticed that she was even paler than usual. I looked at my father, but he seemed intent on his meal, his eyes looking firmly down at his plate. I turned back to my mother.

"What's the matter?" I asked. "What's happened to Oswald?"

Mother said nothing. It was Father who spoke.

"He's ... in hospital," he said quietly. Then he carried on eating.

I stared at him, stunned.

"In hospital?" I echoed. "Why? Where? In France? Was he wounded? Was he badly hurt?"

"Everything's in order," said Father, and continued eating, though I noticed he only took very small mouthfuls and spent a long time chewing, as if he was having difficulty swallowing what he was eating.

"How can it be in order?" I demanded. "What happened to Oswald?"

"Please, Jack, I'd prefer we didn't speak of it," said my mother in a faint voice.

"But he's my brother!" I insisted. "Surely I have a right to know what's happened to him? Is he disabled? Blind? That poison gas is dirty stuff..."

"Your mother has requested that we do not discuss this matter," snapped Father. "Can't you see that it upsets her? We do not wish to talk about Oswald. He is safe and out of harm's way. That is all you need to know. Now let that be an end of it."

With that he continued eating his meal in the same almost reluctant way as before. Mother sat, her plate untouched, her pale face set and her hands pressed together as if in silent prayer.

The rest of the meal was a disaster. The three of us ate in silence. Though when I say "ate" that's a bit of an exaggeration. Mother just pushed her food around her plate with her knife and fork. Father ate ever smaller mouthfuls, taking ages to swallow each one, but acting like a man who was forced to do so as a kind of punishment.

Question after question whirled around my head. What had happened to Oswald? How badly was he injured? Where was he – in France or in England? What had happened to him? Had he been blown up? Shot? Gassed? When had it happened? Who had done it to him? Why hadn't anyone told me earlier?

As soon as the meal was over, I made my apologies to my parents and said I needed an early night. I could tell by their manner that they were relieved that they wouldn't be forced to spend the rest of the evening with me, with my unasked questions bubbling under the whole time, waiting to burst out and cause them even greater distress.

I hurried up to Nanna's rooms and found her sitting up in her chair, reading a book.

"Hello, Nanna," I said, greeting her with a kiss. "I'm sorry I've called so late. I hope I haven't interrupted you going to bed?"

"I rarely sleep much at nights these days," said Nanna. "I do most of my sleeping during the day. One of the least attractive aspects of getting ancient."

"Nonsense," I told her. "I'll never think of you as ancient. Just gently matured, like one of Father's best wines."

"You young flatterer," said Nanna. "So, come on, Jack. You haven't called just to pass the time of day. What's the matter?"

"What's happened to Oswald?" I blurted out.

There was a difficult silence as Nanna looked at me, as if weighing up what to tell me.

Then she said, "I take it your father and mother haven't told you?"

"They refused even to speak about him, except to say that he's in hospital," I said. "But when I asked why, I was told in no uncertain terms he is not a subject for discussion."

Again, Nanna was silent, but this time she looked away from me, studying the photographs on her mantelpiece. We were all there. Me, Father, Mother, Grandfather and Oswald.

"He's in hospital just outside London," she said at last.

"I know he's in hospital," I insisted, "but how was he injured? How bad a state is he in?"

Finally she said quitely, "The army doctor who called to see your father and mother said he was suffering from something called 'shell shock'. I believe it's a nervous disorder."

Shell shock. No wonder Father hadn't wanted to talk about it. Cowardice, some of the generals called it. Loss of nerve.

"When did it happen?" I asked. "A month ago," said Nanna.

A whole month, and no one had written anything to me about it!

"Which hospital is he in?" I asked.

"Why?" asked Nanna.

"I want to go and see him," I said. "Find out how he is."

"Do you think that's a good idea? I don't think your parents would readily give their permission," she said quietly.

"I wasn't thinking of asking them," I said.

Nanna gave a smile. "The same Jack as ever," she said. "Breaking the rules. Going against orders."

"He is my brother," I said. "Who knows, I might even be able to help him get over this ... shell shock."

I spent the next day at home, but it a was very sombre affair. The business of Oswald hung over Mother and Father like a dark cloud. Because they didn't want to talk about him we spent most of our time together in a sort of silence, talking about things like the weather. When I could I retreated to Nanna's rooms to take tea with her and talk. It was the only time I felt anything like normality.

That evening I told my parents that I was going to Farnborough the next day to report to my commanding officers, and receive further orders before returning to the Front. It was a lie, but I knew they wouldn't like to hear where I was really going. Nanna had given me the address of Oswald's hospital, which was at Palace Green near Kensington Gardens in London. Apparently it was a hospital set up by Lord Knutsford specifically for officers suffering from shell shock, or what the doctors termed "war neurosis".

I caught the train to London, and then a taxi to the hospital. It was a fine building, set in beautiful grounds overlooking Palace Gardens. The nurse on duty at reception was surprised at my arriving unannounced.

"Yes, I'm sorry," I apologized. "I've only just got back from the Front myself, and I'm due to report back for duty tomorrow, so I'm afraid there was no time for me to contact you first. But when I heard about my brother being here, I thought I really had to visit him. I hope that seeing me might even help him."

The nurse listened and then said, "I'd better have a word with his doctor first. Usually we like the patients to spend their time here on their own, coming to terms with their condition."

"I promise I won't be any bother at all," I said.

"Then if you'd just take a seat while I check with Dr Farrell," she said, indicating a chair.

I sat down and took stock of the surroundings. Although the building outside was architecturally ornate, inside it was austere. Very few things in the way of decorations. Hardly any pictures. No photographs. I wondered if the medical staff were trying to keep that sort of thing away from the patients in case it triggered off something. I was still sitting reflecting on this when the nurse returned.

"Dr Farrell says you can see your brother," she said. "But only for a few moments. He needs all the rest he can get."

"I promise I won't overstay my welcome," I said.

I followed her down a corridor. The place was eerily quiet. Now and then, as we passed a partly closed door, I heard the sound of sobbing. From one of the rooms, I heard the sounds of muffled screams, as if someone was trying to call out but had a gag stuffed in their mouth. Then I noticed that the door had a key in the lock. This whole place gave me the creeps.

The nurse stopped at a door and tapped at it, then opened it. I followed her into the room. For a moment I wondered whose room we were in. I didn't recognize the man sitting in the chair by the window. I was about to say to the nurse, "Excuse me, but I think there's some mistake. You've brought me into someone else's room," when she said gently to the man in the chair, "Your brother is here, Mr Fairfax."

The man in the chair looked up at me, and I nearly fell to

the floor in shock. It was Oswald right enough, but it took me a second look to make sure.

Oswald was only two years older than me, but this man looked at least 40, with lines across his face, and white and grey streaks in his hair. Oswald had been a tall, upright boy, with a backbone stiff as a ramrod – like a soldier on parade – and prone to being a bit podgy due to a liking for too much pudding. This man was skeleton-thin, bent over, his chest sunken. His eyes were sunken, too, staring blue from black holes in a deathly white face.

The man finally forced himself to look directly at me. "Jack," he said.

His voice, too, had changed. Where before it was loud and bellowing, made so by shouting orders at the junior boys at school, now it was thin and reedy.

"I'll leave you two together," said the nurse.

I sat down on the chair opposite Oswald.

"How are you, old chap?" I asked. "I hear you've been ill."

Oswald nodded. "It's a bad business, Jack," he said. "A bad business."

With that he fell silent, his eyes going down to look at his knees. The silence continued.

I looked around the room. It was neatly, but sparsely, furnished. Clean. Orderly. Again no photographs or pictures. No flowers. None of the usual things you expected to find in a hospital room.

"So," I said, after the silence had gone on for what seemed like ages, "what happened?"

The sound of my voice seemed to remind Oswald that I was in the room with him, and he struggled back from being lost in thought into some kind of waking.

"Do you remember Father telling us about the Battle of Klips Drift?" he asked.

"Only about the first hundred times he told us," I laughed.

Oswald didn't laugh back.

"Of course," I said, in a more serious tone.

The Battle of Klips Drift had been Father's finest hour when he was fighting in the Boer War against the Afrikaners. It had taken place in 1900.

"The Boers were entrenched in a position just north of Klips Drift," said Oswald, telling me the story as if I hadn't heard it before. "Father was with the Greys, plus a squadron of the 6th Dragoons, and the Carabiniers in the 1st Brigade. Cavalry. All on horseback. They had to wait for the transport column to arrive. They waited south of Kimberley, just inside the Orange Free State border."

"I know," I said, puzzled. I wasn't sure why Oswald was telling me this. I'd heard the story from Father time after time as I'd been growing up.

"When they arrived at their objective, the Boer positions at Klips Drift, they made a cavalry charge against them. Because of the speed of the attack, and also because of the dust thrown up by the horses' hooves, they were a very difficult target for the Boer marksmen."

"I know," I said again.

"Father said it was an absolutely classic cavalry manoeuvre," said Oswald. "The front rank of each squadron armed with lances as well as swords and carbines. The Boers were overwhelmed. They left their position in the protection of the Drift and ran for it. That meant the road to Kimberley was now open, and Father and the rest of the cavalry were able to ride into Kimberley and occupy the town. It was a major victory."

"It was," I nodded. "But I don't see what it has to do with us today?"

Oswald lifted his head and looked me straight in the eyes, and now I could see tears starting to tremble on his eyelids.

"Before I went to the Front, Father told me always to use the classic manoeuvres, just as the Regiment had done at Klips Drift, and I would win my encounters with the enemy, as he had done, and my men would come home safely. But, Jack, there was no way there could be any sort of classic manoeuvre in that mud."

He was no longer looking at me, but looking into somewhere inside his own head, some awful memory. "Horses? Cavalry? Dust from their hooves?" He laughed harshly. "No horse could even move in that mud! I've seen horses and donkeys and mules stuck so deep they were nearly drowning in mud and water. I've seen shrapnel take off all four of a horse's legs in one horrifying salvo. The poor beast lay there, screaming – and don't let anyone tell you that animals don't scream. I put a bullet through its brain to put it out of its misery."

I didn't know what to say. I'd never seen Oswald as deeply upset as this before. All my life, during our time as boys at home and our school days, Oswald had been the proper respectable one, the one who did everything that should be done, and never showed his emotions.

"Father has no idea what sort of war this is, Jack. This isn't decent, civilized war. Men on horseback against other men on horseback. Rifles that only allow you or your enemy one shot, and then you have to reload. We are up against guns that fire hundreds of bullets a minute. Bombs that are so big they can destroy a small town. Poison gas. Water. Mud.

"We are treading on our own dead comrades every time we go into attack. The ground and the walls of the trenches are held up by the decomposing bodies of men I have known and liked. Men who followed me because I am their commanding officer. I am a captain in the Royal Scots Dragoon Guards. They did what I said and I carried out the orders of my superior officers. I ordered those men over the top, time after time after time, and they died, Jack. In their hundreds! They died because they did what I told them to do!"

Suddenly Oswald began to cry. Not just tears but great howling roars of deep pain. There was the sound of hurrying footsteps outside, and then the nurse came swiftly into the room and went over to Oswald.

"Captain Fairfax," she said gently, and she put her hands on Oswald's shoulders.

I sat there, looking at my brother as he rocked backwards and forwards on his chair in mental anguish, the nurse holding him, restraining him gently.

She looked at me and said, "I think it might be better if you go. We will give him something to help him sleep. That often helps, but he has a great deal of trouble sleeping."

I'm not surprised, with the brutal images in his mind, I thought. The nightmares Oswald must suffer. The memories that must come back to haunt him in his sleep as soon as his eyes close.

I nodded to her, and got up.

"Will you come and see him again?" the nurse asked me. "I'm sure your visit will have helped him."

"How?" I asked, baffled.

"Sometimes talking about the horrors the patients have experienced can be the first step on the road to recovery," she said.

"I'll do my best," I said. "But I'm off back to the Front in a day or so, and I'm not sure what the future holds."

I turned back to Oswald, but he was lost to me, just

rocking on his chair, his eyes shut tight and his hands firmly over his ears as if trying to block out all sights and sounds.

"I'll see you again, Oswald," I said. "I hope you feel better soon."

As I walked back down that corridor, I kicked myself mentally for saying those last words. In view of Oswald's condition, they seemed so inadequate. But I just didn't know what else to say.

I left the hospital, and went back to the War.

By the time I got to Farnborough they had my replacement
De Hav2 ready for me, and I set off across the Channel. In
the late afternoon I landed back at St Omer. As I came in
to land I saw the airfield was full of planes. I was looking
forward to meeting up with the chaps again and I wondered
if Alan would mind if I told him about what had happened
to Oswald. I knew that Mother and Father wouldn't like it
being spread around, but I was still feeling so shocked at how
Oswald had been in that hospital that part of me needed to
share it with someone, just to get it off my chest.

Oofy Richards was the first person I saw as I walked
into our hut. He beamed when he spotted me. "Jack! I
thought you'd have had more sense than to come back to
this hellhole! But the bright lights of London couldn't keep
you, eh?"

"No chance!" I said with a grin. "The fine food, the luxury
accommodation, the friendly Hun shooting at you every day?
How could life back in England compete with that?!"

I looked around the hut, at the other chaps sitting in
their chairs, ready and waiting for the command to go, and

a few of them waved a hand in greeting. But Alan wasn't in the room. I guessed he was either in the mess sorting out some food, or perhaps he'd gone back to our digs at "the hotel".

"Where's Alan?" I asked.

There was an awkward pause, then Oofy said, "I'm afraid he bought it yesterday."

I looked at him in disbelief.

"Alan?" I said, stunned.

Oofy nodded.

"Anyway," he continued, his voice chirpier, "the weather's been brightening up lately, so..."

"I don't want to hear about the damned weather!" I stormed angrily. "I want to know what happened to Alan! How did he go? Was he shot down? Who did it?" My voice must have risen to a shout without my realizing it, because I heard the voice of Major Sanders snap out from behind me, "What the devil's going on here?"

I turned and faced him.

"I've just found out that Alan Dixon has been killed," I said, "and I'm trying to find out how it happened."

"He was shot down by the Hun," snapped Sanders. "That's it."

"No it isn't!" I shouted back angrily. "How did it happen? Where?"

Beside me, Oofy shuffled his feet unhappily.

Sanders glared back at me, and then he said, "You will come into my office, Lieutenant Fairfax."

I followed Sanders out into the operations hut next door. As we came in, a sergeant stood up from his desk and approached Sanders, holding a piece of paper in his hand, but Sanders waved him away.

"Not at the moment," he said. "I am not to be interrupted for the next three minutes."

With that, Sanders walked into his office. I followed him in.

"Shut the door," he said.

I could tell from his manner that I was in for a roasting. "Sir..." I began, determined to get my explanation in first.

"Silence!" snapped Sanders. "Ordinarily I would not even give you the benefit of this talk, Fairfax, but I understand that you and Dixon had been friends for a long time."

"Since we were six years old, sir," I said. "We met at prep school."

Sanders nodded, but his firm expression didn't change.

"You have just broken one of the unwritten laws of the Flying Corps – trying to get a fellow pilot to talk in detail about the death of a colleague."

I bowed my head apologetically. It was true that there was an unspoken agreement that we didn't talk openly about it when one of us "bought it". It was as if by not talking about it, it would stop it happening to us.

The view of the Top Brass was that dwelling on such

things would "lower our morale" and make us less eager to fight. For that reason, there were never any empty chairs at our briefing sessions. When a man died, a chair was removed, until such time as his replacement arrived.

"I'm sorry, sir," I said. "I admit that I lost my head. As I said, Alan Dixon is ... was ... my best friend in the world. We have been together for as long as I can remember."

"That may be," said Sanders. "But the morale of this squadron is my responsibility, and I will not allow any of my pilots to do anything to undermine that. Is that clear?"

"Yes, sir," I nodded.

"Good," he said. "However, in view of these particular circumstances, I can tell you that Dixon died bravely. He was lost during an air battle with Von Klempter's outfit. I believe it was Von Klempter himself who was responsible."

So, the German I'd ridiculed as "the flying banana" had shot down Alan. The same man who'd downed me. But I had lived.

"The other pilots reported that Dixon took out four Huns before he was shot down," added Sanders. "He was an excellent pilot and a brave warrior. I have written to his parents to tell them so."

"Yes, sir," I said. But there was one more thing I had to find out. "How did he die?"

"I've just told you," replied Sanders. "He was shot down by Von Klempter."

"Yes, but ... was his plane intact?" I finally forced myself to say the words. "Did he burn?"

Sanders said nothing for a moment, but I could see the turmoil behind his eyes. Finally, he said, "That's all you need to know, Lieutenant Fairfax. You are dismissed."

Deep down I felt myself go cold, but I stood to attention, saluted smartly, and left the office.

Oofy was waiting for me outside, looking miserable.

"Is everything all right, Jack?" he asked. "I'm sorry, I didn't mean to land you in trouble like that."

I forced a smile and clapped him on the shoulder.

"You didn't do anything wrong, old boy. It was my fault entirely," I said. "I'm sorry I lost my rag the way I did. I wouldn't hurt you for the world. Forgive me?" And I held out my hand to him.

Oofy grinned as he took my hand and shook it.

"Nothing to forgive," he said. Then he added, awkwardly, "But I am most awfully sorry about Alan."

"I know," I said. "Thanks." Once again I forced myself to smile. "I'd better go and check my crate. I want to make sure it's ready for action tomorrow."

"Good egg!" Oofy replied.

I watched Oofy head back towards our hut, then I turned and walked towards where our planes were parked. I hoped that no one was around. As I walked I could feel my cheeks wet with tears. I bit my lip to try to stop them. Grown chaps don't cry. Alan would hate to see me crying like this. I'd be letting the side down. But when it came to it, there was no side, just friends.

I felt hollow inside. Worst of all was that I now knew that Alan had died in a burning plane. I remembered the fear I'd felt when I thought my plane was going to catch fire. I couldn't shake the thought of Alan – what was it the Germans called it? Gebrannt. Burnt. Well now I had a score to settle. I was going to get Von Klempter.

The next day I was ready to get up into the air again and take on the Hun, hoping that Von Klempter and his "flying circus" would be up there, but instead our whole squadron were summoned to a briefing in the mess. It was unusual for us to be taken off flying duties en masse just for a pep talk, so I guessed there was something big in the air. I was right.

Major Sanders waited until we were all sitting quietly and attentively, and then he began.

"Chaps, I don't need to tell you that the war on the ground has been at a stalemate for some time. Well, tomorrow that is going to change. The Army Top Brass have decided to go for a major push on the Somme. Those of you who've been up will have noticed our big guns have been laying an even heavier bombardment on the enemy than usual."

I assumed the increased bombardment the CO was talking about had been going on while I had been back in England, because I hadn't been aware of it when I'd been up in the air. Though when you're at 10,000 feet, as you battle with the enemy twisting and turning in the sky, it's difficult to concentrate on what's happening on the ground.

"Today, you're standing down and you're to check your machines. Tomorrow's going to be our big day. Meanwhile 21 Squadron are going on offensive duty today. They're going to add to the Hun's worries by carrying out a bombing raid."

A bombing raid usually meant a two-seater going over enemy positions, with the crewman in the rear seat throwing bombs out of the plane on to the enemy below. It was a risky business as they had to fly low enough to make sure the bombs were on target, yet not so low that they ran into flak from the German anti-aircraft guns.

"The plan for tomorrow is that the big bombardment from our heavy guns will begin at 0730 hours. They will pound the German lines in a concentrated attack until 0800. As the barrage lifts, the infantry will move forward at speed, cross the barbed wire and attack the enemy in their forward trenches. The generals believe that the Huns will still be in their deep dugouts, recovering from the heavy bombardment, and won't have time to get to their machine-guns.

"At the same time, to ensure further cover for the ground troops, bombers will fly over and attack the German positions behind the front line. Your job will be to escort and protect those bombers. If this push is successful, as I'm sure it will be, it will decimate the enemy, pushing the Germans back so far and so fast that they will be forced to surrender.

"So, gentlemen, prepare for tomorrow, and for what could be the beginning of the last days of this war."

As we headed out of the mess hall, I gave Oofy a humourless grin.

"One more push, eh, Oofy!" I said. "I wish I'd had a pound for every time we'd been promised that."

"Now don't be a cynic, Jack," said Oofy. "The Top Brass have special intelligence. They know things that we don't, about the Germans and their weaknesses, and that sort of thing. They know what they're doing. I, for one, am looking forward to doing anything that gets this war over with so I can get home." He hesitated, looked round to make sure no one else was within earshot, then added, "The thing is, I'm engaged to be married."

"My goodness, Oofy, who'd marry you?" I exclaimed. I mean, Oofy was a nice enough chap, but hardly what I'd describe as handsome. He had a head that went to a point at the top, and no real chin to speak of. His head struck me as looking like a rugby ball perched on his neck.

Oofy looked at me, put out.

"I'll have you know my fiancée, Gladys, is a woman of great taste," he said. "Everyone says so."

"Sorry, old chap," I said with a smile. "Just joking. I'm sure you'll be very happy together."

I spent the rest of the day going over my De Hav with one of the mechanics. When we ran into the Hun tomorrow, as I was certain we would, I didn't want to be put out of action on account of any mechanical failures. Nor did I want the wings collapsing on me. They'd felt a little edgy as I'd flown over the Channel the previous day, so we worked to ensure the rigging lines were firm and the wooden struts were properly lined up. Then we went through the engine and fuel lines, and lastly I checked the Lewis gun and ammunition. Whatever happened tomorrow, I was going to be ready.

The next morning at 0715 hours, the whole of our squadron was assembled on the field: fourteen single-seater fighter planes, and six two-seaters, with their bomb loads. It was early July, but the morning seemed particularly chill, and I knew it would be even colder at 10,000 feet, so I'd made sure I was dressed to withstand the cold. I had on my leather flying jacket with its big fleecy collar, a woolly scarf, thick gloves, fleece-lined flying boots, and my leather flying cap.

The bombardment of our heavy guns began on the dot at 0730 hours. Even from miles away we not only heard them, we felt them – the ground shaking under our feet as they fired and sent their huge shells raining down on the German front lines.

At the whistle we "mounted up", clambering into the cockpits of our planes. It always struck me as odd that we still used the language of the cavalry, even though we used planes instead of horses. Father would have felt at home here.

At 0740 hours we started our engines. The six two-seaters that were to carry out the bombing raid, being larger and slower, took off first and headed in a southerly direction. They were to keep behind our own lines for safety, and wait to rendezvous with us, their escort.

As the bombardment ended, exactly at 0800, we were flying across the front line, heading for the German trenches. Below me I could see our ground troops emerging from the trenches and heading into no-man's-land, hurrying forward. Even from this relatively low height they looked like ants, swarming over the grey mud. I now knew what conditions were like down there at ground level – I'd seen them up close for myself. But I could only begin to guess at the horrors that Oswald had experienced, and for such a long time, that had finally broken his spirit and driven him mad.

From below I heard the chatter of rapid machine-gunfire, and I knew it had to be the Germans firing because our men only had rifles. But I didn't have time to look closer because I saw the shapes of planes in the far distance, coming from the German lines. The enemy had been alerted about us and were on their way.

Our two-seaters had already started their bombing of the German lines, dropping down low, the observer in the rear of the plane leaning out and sending the bombs hurtling down towards the ground. As we had planned, nine of us lifted up to 12,000 feet and headed in formation towards the oncoming enemy planes. The plan was to head them off and keep them busy at a distance, while the two-seaters continued with their bombing work, protected by the remaining six members of our squadron. As soon as the two-seaters had finished, they were to turn and head back home, the six escorts staying with them to protect them against any stray German who'd managed to get past us.

As we neared the approaching German planes, I felt a thrill of excitement as I recognized their distinctive bright yellow wings and bodies, with their black crosses at the end of the wings, on the tail, and on the side. Von Klempter and his cronies had come looking for more victims. But today would be the day that Von Klempter would meet his fate. I could feel the desire for revenge burning inside me and I wanted to yell out loud, "Come on, Von Klempter! Face me!"

The planes from both sides began firing before we were in range of one another. It had now become a standard tactic, firing a burst to try and make your opponent react, throw him off his track.

I scanned their formation, searching for the huge face on the propeller mounting that was Von Klempter's trademark. At first I couldn't see it, and I felt a sense of disappointment that Von Klempter might have decided not to go up with his pals. But then I spotted it, in the middle of the pack, and I turned and flew down, aiming to fly beneath them and come up at Von Klempter from below.

One of the German pilots saw the direction I was heading in and turned and followed me down, opening up with a burst of gunfire as he did so, but I caught the movement out of the corner of my eye and managed to turn aside at the last minute, and the line of tracer missed the front of my plane by inches.

I cautioned myself to be careful, not to let my intent to get Von Klempter blind me to the fact that the rest of the German squadron were superb pilots in their own right. Any one of them could shoot me down if I didn't keep my wits about me.

The air battle was already in full swing, the yellow German planes hurtling this way and that, guns blazing. Our own planes ducked and dived and fired back, every man desperate to get an accurate, or at least a lucky, shot, before his adversary could get a sighting on him.

Two planes were already going down, both of them in flames – one German, one British – leaving a trail of black smoke behind them as they hurtled groundwards. I hoped for their sake that both pilots were already dead. No one wished being burned alive on anyone.

Another German fired a burst at me, and I felt my machine shudder as his bullets hit the woodwork behind me. I put the De Hav's nose down and took it into a short dive, then flew back up, turning as I did so, enough to bring me on to the enemy's tail. I fired off a burst and saw his tail fall to pieces, and the next second he sank like a stone, going into a spin, the wings whirling around like a spinning top.

Another German came for me, and this time I flew higher, with a quick upward glance first to make sure I wasn't on a collision course with anyone. There was one plane above me, bright yellow, and as it turned towards me I saw again that familiar face painted on the propeller mounting. Von Klempter!

Unfortunately, the jolt of realization that it was Von Klempter himself delayed my finger on the trigger for just a fraction of a second. The German ace flipped neatly away from my line of bullets, turning left, then going higher. I followed him up to 15,000 feet. It was colder up here, much colder, and I was glad I had my sheepskin gloves on or my hands would have been too cold to operate the gun.

I fired off another burst, but again the wily German avoided my gunfire, this time wheeling to the right, my bullets passing harmlessly beneath his left wing as it went up and he turned. He seemed to have some kind of sixth sense, as if he knew what I was going to do next. Suddenly he turned so sharply that I thought I was going to run into him head-on, and I pulled back on the joystick to lift my machine up. Too late. I heard the rack-ack-ack explosion of his guns, and I felt a searing pain in my right shoulder. The whole right side of my body went numb, but just for a second, and then the pain kicked in. I could feel my shirt inside my jacket starting to get wet around the shoulder and chest, and I knew I'd been shot. Von Klempter had let off a burst just above the level of my cockpit and one bullet had gone straight through my leather jacket.

It hurt like hell. Every movement of my right hand on the controls sent a jolt of pain through my upper body. I wondered how bad the wound was. How much blood had I lost already?

I was just trying to recover myself, regain control of my machine, when I saw Von Klempter coming back at me from the left-hand side, coming to finish me off. I gritted my teeth against the pain and put the De Hav into a dive. I was just in time because a burst from Von Klempter's guns tore through the sky over my head as I dropped down. If I'd delayed even by a second I'd have been riddled with bullets.

"This is no good, Jack!" I shouted at myself angrily. "He's getting you! You're supposed to be getting him!" I saw the shadow of Von Klempter's plane spiral down from above me, and guessed he was intending to come in from behind me and shoot me. Immediately I went into a further dive to take me lower. As before, Von Klempter followed me down, sure now that he had me. He must have guessed he'd hit me, and maybe thought I had lost enough blood to start losing consciousness. I began to spiral down, and then suddenly, abruptly, pulled the joystick back hard and soared up, heading straight into his flight path.

My manoeuvre caught Von Klempter by surprise and he had to turn sharply to avoid crashing into me. Although he fired off a burst, it was a reflex action because he was more concerned about getting out of my way.

I was now above him, at about 17,000 feet, and I was getting colder, which made handling my plane more difficult. The pain in my shoulder was spreading across my chest. I knew I couldn't hold out much longer. I had to do something to stop the loss of blood before I lost consciousness.

The chatter of rapid machine-gun fire coming from behind me told me that Von Klempter had recovered and followed me, and was on my tail again, trying to finish me off. Once more I put the De Hav's nose down and dived beneath his tracer of bullets, and turned, then turned quickly again to put myself on a level course with Von Klempter.

Now I was heading straight for his plane broadside on, working the trigger as I did so ... and to my shock, nothing happened. I knew I wasn't out of bullets. The firing mechanism had jammed! When he'd hit me some of his bullets must have also struck my gun.

I cursed aloud. Here I was, in an air battle with a leading German ace, and I was wounded, losing blood, and without a gun.

I saw Von Klempter soar past me, then go higher, and as

he did so I was certain he turned his head towards me and smiled. He knew from the fact that my guns hadn't fired at him that there must be something wrong. He had a sitting duck for a target.

I watched him circle above me, like a hunting eagle circling its prey, and then he dived, swooping towards me. He didn't fire straightaway. He knew that he didn't have to. I was unarmed, helpless. All he had to do was draw as near as he wanted, then shoot me. Or maybe let me get away just a little and begin to head for home, then shoot me down as I fled.

But I wasn't going to head for home – though I let him think so. I turned and began to fly towards our own lines, weaving from side to side, twisting and turning as if I was trying to throw him off. I could hear the sound of his engine as he gained on me. He let off a burst from his guns, but because I was taking an erratic path as I flew, he missed. Nearer he came, determined not to miss the next time, determined to gain another kill to add to his list of victories.

Suddenly I manoeuvred, joystick hard back, full right rudder, then twisted round to face him directly, and flew straight for him. As I'd hoped, the move shocked him – a man with no guns heading straight for him, set on an instant air collision.

My life or death now depended on what he did next: whether he went up, or down and tried to go beneath me. If he went upwards, then I had lost.

He went down, putting his plane into a dive to avoid me, and I dived too, but turning to my left as I did so, pulling back on the joystick at the last moment and leaning far left, almost putting my machine sideways into the sky.

I felt a terrifying crash and heard a tearing sound, and then my plane was spinning and I had to battle to control it. Desperately I fought with the rudders, using my feet against the bars with all my might. My plane gave a last lurch, and then began to fly in a straight line again. Out of the corner of my eye I saw Von Klempter's yellow plane heading out of control down towards the ground, one of its wings flapping uselessly in the wind, before tearing away from the plane completely.

I had done it. I'd rammed Von Klempter's right wing with my undercarriage, my wheels smashing into it and tearing it half away from the fuselage of his plane. In so doing I'd torn off at least one of my wheels, if not both of them. Landing was going to be an interesting experience.

I looked around me at the sky. The survivors of Von Klempter's squadron had decided to head for home, and my own flying pals who'd lived through this encounter were also now turning and heading for our own lines.

Our battle in the skies above the Somme was over. I was still alive, and I'd had my revenge for Alan's death – as well as paying something back for all our other boys that Von Klempter had shot down.

I could feel myself growing weaker as I approached the airfield. The loss of blood from my wounds was starting to affect me. I had to fight to concentrate if I was going to land this machine successfully using just my one good arm. After all that had gone on in the air, it would be stupid to kill myself landing.

I came in lower and lower towards the field, gritting my teeth against the pain down my right side.

The green grass came rushing up towards me and I pulled back on the joystick with my left arm as the plane hit the ground with a bone-jarring crunch that sent pain coursing through my whole body. The plane leapt back up into the air, then came down again as I pushed the joystick forward. I bounced a few more times across the field, and then finally the plane came to rest at a cock-eyed angle, listing heavily to one side, the right wing tips digging into the ground.

I tried to drag myself out of the cockpit, but the effort was too great. I heard the sound of men running across the grass towards me, then a voice saying, "Are you all right, old chap?"

I looked into the face of one of the ground crew, and gave him a grin. I was alive. Von Klempter was dead.

"Never better," I said.

EPILOGUE
NOVEMBER 1918

Von Klempter's bullets had made a nasty mess of my shoulder and I spent four months on sick leave before returning to the Front.

The Battle of the Somme didn't end the War, which went on for another two and a bit years, until finally, just a week ago, the Germans surrendered.

Incredibly, I survived. I don't know how. So many others didn't. Some died after a few months, some only lasted a few days. Oofy never made it home to marry his fiancée; he died just two days before the Germans surrendered, shot down while flying on a reconnaissance mission. Very few fighter pilots survived the War right to the end as I did.

My first act on returning to England was to call on Alan's family to offer my condolences. They, in turn, offered their condolences for my own family's losses.

In August 1918 Oswald died in the hospital. At that time I was still in France. I had a letter from Nanna telling me that he'd choked on some tablets. The official verdict was accidental death. My own feeling, though I didn't tell this to anyone in my family, was that Oswald couldn't cope with the horror he'd experienced, and that he'd taken his own life with an overdose.

The shock of Oswald's death hit Father particularly badly. Oswald had stood for everything that Father held dear: tradition, the good name and the future of the Fairfax family, the honour of the Regiment. Although there could be no doubt that Oswald had been a brave soldier at the Front, to be invalided home with shell shock had been a grave blow for Father. Despite his love for Oswald, I could tell that, for him, it sullied the family name. His hope had been that Oswald would return to his former health, and rejoin the Regiment, at least for a while. Instead, Oswald died. For Father, it was just too much for him to take. A week after Oswald's death, Father suffered a heart attack and died.

Shortly after Father's death, my plane was shot down during a battle with the Hun. I suffered only minor injuries, a broken leg and arm, but enough for me to be invalided back to England.

And so, at the age of 21, I have returned home to England and Bowness Hall as the new Lord Fairfax. It feels strange to me, being responsible for the people of the villages that make up the Fairfax estate. Men and women who knew me when I was just a small boy now call me "My Lord" and "Master". They look to me to give security to their lives. I know that I must not let them down. That was one of the things the War taught me: when you have power, and the lives and safety of other people are in your hands, you have a human duty to take care of them. I learnt that the hard way in a time of war. As the new Lord Fairfax, I hope I will not be found wanting in times of peace.

HISTORICAL NOTE

When the First World War began in 1914 aeroplanes were still a relatively recent invention. The first flight in a heavier-than-air machine was made by the brothers Orville and Wilbur Wright of the United States in 1903. The first cross-Channel flight from Calais to Dover was made six years later by Louis Blériot, in 1909, just five years before the War started.

At first there was great resistance among the senior officers in the British military to the idea of using aeroplanes as a military force. Many thought that they were a fad that wouldn't last. However, aware that other countries such as Germany and France had already taken the lead in aeroplane technology, reluctantly the British military authorities agreed to consider the matter.

In 1911 the Air Battalion of the Royal Engineers was formed, and in 1912 the Royal Flying Corps was set up, which incorporated the Air Battalion. The Navy had also decided to set up its own air service, and so the Royal Naval Air Service came into being in 1912, although it was not given an official seal of approval until 1914.

Many of the first planes were unreliable and as dangerous to the men who flew them as they were to the enemy. Flimsily constructed of wood and cloth with wire rigging, often they did not have the strength to hold together under the stresses of flying. Fabric could be stripped from the wing during a long dive; undercarriages would break off during landing. Many pilots died in training, before they ever got to meet the enemy.

As the War progressed, both sides worked to develop a fighting aeroplane that was superior to those of the enemy. In a short space of time new machines appeared with new forms of guns. The advantage swung this way and that. First the Germans had the superior position with the Fokker monoplanes, then the Allies matched them with the British De Havilland DH2 and the French Nieuport.

These, in turn, were superseded by the German Albatross, which dominated the skies, and was the favoured flying weapon of the legendary Baron Manfred Von Richthofen.

Von Richthofen was known as "the Red Baron" because his plane was painted completely red. In this book, the fictional character of Von Klempter is based in part on Von Richthofen.

By 1917 it looked as if the air war had been won by the Germans as they decimated the ranks of the RFC. (The average life expectancy of a fighter pilot in the RFC at that time was estimated at less than two weeks.)

Then, late in 1917, two new planes appeared: the British SE5A and the French Spad XIII. Both of these planes were fast and strong, with the Spad having the advantage of two Vickers guns in the fuselage. Gradually they began to turn the tide. The tide was turned completely with the appearance of the Sopwith Camel in July 1917. The Camel had a rotary engine, two Vickers guns, and excellent aerobatic qualities.

But it wasn't just the machines that won the battles in the air, it was the men who flew them. Although a pilot's life in the First World War was generally a short one, some mastered the technique of aerial fighting and survival, and their names live on in the history of aerial combat. Baron Manfred Von Richthofen may have been the most well known of the First World War fighters, but both sides had their share of aces.

For the RFC, the primary aces were Mick Mannock VC, James McCudden VC and Albert Ball. Mannock was Britain's top ace, who only started flying in 1917 but had 73 victories before he died in 1918 in aerial combat. James McCudden scored 57 victories before he was killed in July 1918. Albert Ball was 20 years old when he was shot down and killed in May 1917. By the time of his death he had 44 victories to his credit.

As well as Von Richthofen, German aces included: Oswald Boelcke, the first German ace and creator of many air-fighting techniques, who had scored 40 victories by the time he died in October 1916; Max Immelman, one of the first generation of aces, who had scored 15 victories by the time of his death in June 1916; and Werner Voss, who at one time was almost matching Von Richthofen with 22 British planes shot down in 21 days. He died in September 1917.

Manfred Von Richthofen was shot down and killed in April 1918. He had a tally of 80 victories.

By the end of the War, the casualty figures of pilots were:

British

6,166 killed

7,245 wounded

3,212 missing or taken prisoner

German

5,853 killed

7,302 wounded

2,751 missing or taken prisoner

On 1 April 1918 the RFC and RNAS were amalgamated into the Royal Air Force.

THE BATTLE OF THE SOMME – 1916

The first day of the Battle of the Somme, 1 July 1916, was a disaster for the Allies (the British and French). Despite a week of heavy bombardment of the German positions prior to 1 July, during which nearly two million shells were fired, most of the German barbed wire, dugouts, and machine-gun positions were intact. As a result, the British lost 60,000 officers and men on this first day, cut down by a hail of German gunfire, for a gain of 1,000 yards.

The Battle of the Somme continued until 18 November 1916. By the end of it, the Allies had advanced a distance of two miles along a line 15 miles long. The casualty figures for this battle were:

British: 418,000 killed or wounded
French: 194,000 killed or wounded
German: 650,000 killed or wounded.

TIMELINE

1903 First flight in a heavier-than-air machine by Orville and Wilbur Wright.

1907 Henri Farman creates successful biplane.

1909 First cross-Channel flight from Calais to Dover by Louis Blériot. Henri Farman makes first 100-mile flight.

1910 Louis Paulhan wins prize for powered flight from London to Manchester.

1911 First use of aircraft for offensive action by Italians in Libya.

1912 First parachute descent from an aircraft. Royal Flying Corps formed.

June 1914 Assassination of Archduke Ferdinand at Sarajevo. Austria attacks Serbia.

July 1914 Austria and Hungary at war with Russia. August 1914 Germany declares war on Russia and France, and invades Belgium. Great Britain declares war on Germany. First single-seater fighter planes made in Britain.

January 1915 First Zeppelin (giant German airship) raid on

England takes place around Yarmouth. Four people were killed and 16 injured.

1916 First tank used by Heavy Machine Gun Corps (later Royal Tank Corps). First successful British airship built.

July–November 1916 The Battle of the Somme. April 1917 The United States declares war on Germany.

1917 Gotha, a German twin-engined biplane, is the first aircraft designed especially for bombing. November 1918 Allied–German armistice. Kaiser Wilhelm II of Germany abdicates.

1918 Royal Flying Corps (RFC) becomes Royal Air Force (RAF).

June 1919 Treaty of Versailles signed between Allies and Germany.

First World War Combat Planes

BRITISH

Sopwith 1 1– Strutter 2

Weight: 1,308 lbs (empty); 2,223 lbs (loaded)

Maximum speed at 10,000 ft: 87.5 mph

Time taken to climb to 10,000 ft: 29 minutes 30 seconds

Maximum altitude: 16,000 ft

Endurance: 3 hours

Engine: 110hp Clerget

Armament: 2 machine-guns (0.303 inch)

Number built: 5,990

Sopwith Pup

WEIGHT: 856 lbs (empty); 1,225 lbs (loaded)

MAXIMUM SPEED AT 10,000 FT: 106 mph

TIME TAKEN TO CLIMB TO 10,000 FT: 14 minutes 25 seconds

MAXIMUM ALTITUDE: 17,500 ft

ENDURANCE: 3 hours

ENGINE: 130hp Le Rhone

ARMAMENT: Vickers or Lewis 0.303 inch machine-gun

NUMBER BUILT: 1,770

De Havilland DH2 (also known as Airco DH2)

Weight: 943 lbs (empty); 1,441 lbs (loaded)

Maximum speed at 10,000 ft: 93 mph

Time taken to climb to 6,500 ft: 12 minutes

Maximum altitude: 14,000 ft

Endurance: 2 hours 45 minutes

Engine: 100hp Genome Monosoupape

Armament: Lewis 0.303 inch machine-gun

Number built: 400

GERMAN

Fokker EI

Weight: 787 lbs (empty); 1,238 lbs (loaded)

Maximum speed at 10,000 ft: 82 mph

Time taken to climb to 10,000 ft: over 40 minutes

Maximum altitude: 10,000 ft

Endurance: 1 hour 30 minutes

Engine: Oberusel U0 rotary 80hp

Armament: Forward-firing MG belt-fed machine-gun

Number built: 54

FOKKER EIII

WEIGHT: 878 lbs (empty); 1,342 lbs (loaded)

MAXIMUM SPEED AT 10,000 FT: 88 mph

TIME TAKEN TO CLIMB TO 10,000 FT: over 40 minutes

MAXIMUM ALTITUDE: 12,200 ft

ENDURANCE: 1 hour 30 minutes

ENGINE: Oberusel UI 9 cylinder rotary 100hp

ARMAMENT: 0.312 inch Parabellum or MG machine-gun

NUMBER BUILT: 260

Albatross DII

Weight: 1,367 lbs (empty); 1,954 lbs (loaded)

Maximum speed at 10,000 ft: 109 mph

Time taken to climb to 10,000 ft: 14 minutes 8 seconds

Maximum altitude: 17,060 ft

Endurance: 1 hour 30 minutes

Engine: 160hp Mercedes

Armament: 2 machine-guns

Number built: not known